For Jason –
may you never need the meteorite spoon.

Every morning Filly and Fergal would wake up and wait for the arguments to start.

Now, all mums and dads argue, of course.

Some argue once in a while: others argue a lot. Some argue through clenched teeth: others open their mouths wide and shout as loud as they can. Some break things when they argue: others don't do any damage at all.

But no parents – not in The Whole History of Parents Arguing – ever argued as much or shouted as loud or broke as many things as Mr and Mrs Thunder.

They could hardly say one word to each other without a row flaring up.

For example, if Mr Thunder looked out of the window and said, 'Oh, look at all those clouds. I think it's going to rain today,' Mrs Thunder would look out and say, 'You must be blind, you nincompoop! There's a ray of sunshine over there! It's going to be hot and sunny!'

And there'd be an argument!

Or, on the other hand, if Mrs Thunder looked out of the window and said, 'Oh, what a blue sky. I think it's going to be hot and sunny today,' Mr Thunder would look out and say, 'Open your eyes, you numbskull! There's a cloud over there! It's going to rain!'

And – you've guessed it – there'd be another argument!

Of course, it hadn't always been like this.

When Mr and Mrs Thunder had first met it had been love at first sight. They didn't even raise their voices at each other in those days, let alone shout and throw things.

But now...

Now the Thunder household was a place of bickering and broken things.

Most things in the house had been broken in one argument or another: the china cups had been smashed when Mr Thunder threw them against a wall, the mirror in the bathroom had been cracked when Mrs Thunder hurled her shoe at it (she had been aiming at Mr Thunder's head, but he ducked just in time), the big vase in the hallway had been shattered when...oh, the list goes on and on.

And – because Mr and Mrs Thunder didn't have much money – everything had to be glued back together again.

Hence, a house of 'broken things'.

Needless to say, if Mr and Mrs Thunder argued more than any parents in The Whole History of Parents Arguing, then no children heard as many arguments – not in The Whole History of Children Listening to Parents Arguing – as Filly and Fergal Thunder.

Filly was ten years old, had a shaggy mop of black hair, large, dark eyes and was both very tall and very thin. ('You look like you've been stretched!' Mrs Thunder sometimes told her – which didn't exactly please poor Filly. 'A stretched zebra! That's what you are!')

Mrs Thunder called her daughter a 'stretched zebra' because of the turtle-neck jumper Filly wore. It had black and white stripes going across it, you see, and was so long it reached Filly's knees. Mrs Thunder didn't like the jumper at all (because it was so threadbare and pulled out of shape), but, to be honest, Filly didn't have much choice. With so little money coming into the house (neither Mr Thunder nor Mrs Thunder had jobs), new clothes were out of the question. As were new shoes – which is why the soles of Filly's big black boots had to be glued back on every other day.

Fergal, her brother, was seven years old and, although he had a shaggy mop of black hair and large, dark eyes, he was the opposite of his sister in almost every other way. For example, he was very short for his age. ('Like you've been squashed!' Mr Thunder sometimes told him – which didn't exactly please poor Fergal. 'Squashed into that jumper of yours!')

Indeed, 'squashed into that jumper' is exactly what Fergal looked like. It was a striped jumper (just like Filly's) and Fergal rolled the neck up over his face so that only his eyes were showing. It was as if he was trying to hide inside his jumper like a turtle hides inside its shell. Which, in a way, he was.

You see, the three years that separated Filly from Fergal were important in one respect: Filly could remember a time when Mr and Mrs Thunder *didn't* argue. True, they were only vague memories (after all, Filly was little more than a baby herself), but she could still recall Mr and Mrs Thunder laughing and hugging and calling each other 'my love'.

But Fergal had no such memories. All he had grown up with were things being broken and lots of shouting.

As a result, he hid himself in his jumper and hardly ever spoke. When he did speak it was only two words at a time. Things like, 'Yep, Sis,' or, 'Nope, Sis,' or, 'Sure, Sis.' And his voice was always so empty and sad that Filly (his 'Sis') did everything she could to cheer him (her 'Brov') up.

The first thing she did was start *The Book of Arguments*.

You see, Filly thought that if she treated their parents' arguing like a kind of game – a hobby almost – then Fergal wouldn't get so distressed.

So, concealed behind the wardrobe in Filly and Fergal's bedroom was a big black book. On the front of the book, in large letters, was written THE BOOK OF ARGUMENTS, and then underneath, in smaller letters, 'A Daily Record of the Endless Arguments of Mr and Mrs Thunder'. Inside, it was full of all kinds of information: what the arguments were about, how long they lasted and what got broken. Whatever was broken during an argument usually gave the argument its title. For example, there was 'The Argument that Broke the Frying-pan' (that was three weeks ago), and 'The Argument that Broke the Television' (that was last year – 1 December, to be precise), and, only yesterday, there'd been 'The Argument that Broke the Washing-machine'. (That had been a particularly long argument and the washing-machine made a very loud bang when it broke.)

And so that's what Filly and Fergal's lives were like: nothing but arguments and arguments and even more arguments.

Filly thought, Our lives will always be like this.

But she was wrong!

Because, one day, everything changed.

The day in question was in August.

To be precise: a Wednesday.

To be even more precise than that: five minutes past nine in the morning.

Because it was at that time that Filly was woken by Fergal calling...

— 2 —

'Arguments, Sis!'

Filly's eyes clicked open.

'Arguments, Sis!'

Filly leaned over the edge of her top bunk and looked at Fergal, who was asleep in the bottom one.

He was thrashing about in the throes of a nightmare, twisting and turning, entangling himself in the sheets.

Immediately, Filly jumped out of bed and tried to wake him.

'Buck up, Brov!' she said, shaking his shoulder. 'It's only a nightmare!'

Whenever Fergal was particularly upset by the arguments, he had nightmares. Filly guessed it was yesterday's 'The Argument that Broke the Washing-machine' that had triggered this one. After all, it did last for seven hours and thirty-two minutes and seventeen seconds, and Filly and Fergal had to sit in their bedroom, listening, without anything to eat or drink. They'd been faint with hunger and thirst by the time it was all over.

'Arguments, Sis!'

'Crikey, Brov, please buck up.'

Filly was getting very worried about Fergal. Once before, almost three months ago now (after 'The Argument that Broke the Yucca Plant'), Fergal had got himself into such a state that he'd run down to the cellar and cried and cried for hours and hours.

There was nothing Filly could do to stop him. She told him to 'buck up' and things like that, but it did no good. Fergal just sobbed and sobbed, until his jumper got so wet Filly was afraid it might shrink.

'Come back upstairs, Brov,' she had said.

'Nope, Sis,' Fergal had replied tearfully.

'But why, Brov?'

'Arguments, Sis.'

'So how long are you going to stay down here, Brov?'

'For ever, Sis.'

But, of course, he didn't.

And, for a while, it seemed as if he was coping.

But now the nightmares were back!

Crikey, thought Filly, I hope poor Brov doesn't start crying again. His jumper will shrink for sure next time.

Filly grabbed hold of Fergal's shoulders and shook him so hard a bed-spring went 'TWANG'!

It was the twanging rather than the shaking that woke him.

Filly tried to look as calm as possible.

'What tish-tosh those nightmares of yours are, Brov,' she said, starting to get dressed. 'I bet that's the last one you have. Think so, Brov?'

'Dunno, Sis,' Fergal responded faintly.

'Well, I'm sure it will be. Now, buck up and get dressed. We'll try to get some breakfast before Mum and Dad wake up. I'm still a little hungry from yesterday. You, Brov?'

'Yep, Sis.'

This was their favourite time of the day: that brief period in the morning before their parents woke up. The house was so peaceful then. Filly and Fergal wished it would always stay like this. But it never did. Because before long –

THUMP!

A noise from their parents' bedroom!

Filly noticed Fergal's eyes get very worried above

the neck of his jumper. And he started to frown. A serious, deep frown that made him look older than he was.

'Golly-gosh!' exclaimed Filly brightly. 'That's Mum and Dad getting up already. Now, you know what to do, Brov. Time for the stop-watch. Don't dilly-dally!'

Fergal grabbed a stop-watch from the bedside cabinet. He pressed a button and a second hand started to tick round.

THUMP!

Another noise from the bedroom next door.

Filly pressed her ear to the wall.

'They're putting on their dressing-gowns,' she said. Then asked, 'How long, Brov?'

Fergal showed her the watch.

'Fifty-seven seconds,' noted Filly.

There was a creaking sound as their parents' bedroom door was opened (the door had been broken in 'The Argument that Broke the Hinges', almost two years ago).

Footsteps in the corridor outside.

'That's Mum!' announced Filly.

Sound of another door opening.

'Mum's going into the bathroom.'

Running tap-water.

'She's cleaning her teeth.'

Footsteps right outside their bedroom door.

'Mum's left the bathroom ... She's going downstairs ... Now Dad's leaving the bedroom ... Mum's going to the kitchen ... Dad's going into the bathroom ... Mum's started breakfast ... Dad's cleaning his teeth ... Mum's putting the kettle on ... Dad's leaving the bathroom ... Mum's putting tea in the teapot ... Dad's going downstairs ... THEY'RE BOTH IN THE

— 16 —

KITCHEN, BROV!'

Filly and Fergal gave each other a knowing look.

With their parents now wide awake and in the same room an argument could erupt at any moment.

'How long, Brov?' asked Filly. 'Show me! Chop-chop!'

Fergal turned the watch towards her.

'Oh, I do wish you'd just tell me the time, Brov. Really I do. This is our hobby after all. You're supposed to be taking an interest.'

Still Fergal refused to say the time.

Filly sighed and looked at the watch.

'Five minutes!' she gasped. 'That's a long time, don't you think, Brov?'

Fergal didn't respond. He just sat on the edge of his mattress, staring forlornly at the watch.

'Buck up, Brov!' said Filly, as chirpily as she could. 'Let's go to the top of the stairs. We can hear Mum and Dad better from there. Zip-zip!'

Filly was always saying things like 'don't dilly-dally' and 'chop-chop' and 'zip-zip'. And, sometimes – when she got really excited – she put them all together like this: 'Don't dilly-dally-chop-chop-zip-

zip!' And there were still other times – when she got really, really excited – when she put them all together, but in the wrong order, like this: 'Don't dilly-chop-zip-dally-zip-chop!'

Now, however, she was calm and, as quietly as possible, she and Fergal crept down the corridor, sat at the top of the stairs and peered through the banisters into the kitchen below.

They couldn't actually see their mum and dad. Just their shadows on the floor. Both of them appeared to be sitting at the kitchen table.

'How long, Brov?'

Fergal showed her the watch, but it was too dark

to see.

'Let's get some light on the subject, Brov,' said
Filly, turning on the lamp at the top of the stairs.

A magical blue light illuminated everything.

This was no ordinary lamp, you see. It was in the
shape of the planet Earth. The magical blue light
came from all the swirling oceans and countries.

The lamp was the first thing that Mr and Mrs
Thunder had ever bought for the house and, as
such, it was very special to them. ('It means the
world to me,' Mrs Thunder used to say with a
chuckle – in those days when chuckles still existed
in the household.) So far, The Lamp of the World
was the only thing not to have been damaged in an
argument. Filly dreaded to think what might
happen if it ever did get broken.

'Eight minutes!' gasped Filly, now able to see the
watch. 'That is a long time, Brov!'

And she was right. Usually Mr and Mrs Thunder
started arguing within six minutes of waking up.

And sometimes – like the first argument on 2 July of this year – they actually woke up arguing. On that particular occasion, Mr Thunder had been dreaming about shouting at Mrs Thunder, and Mrs Thunder had been dreaming about shouting at Mr Thunder, and, when they woke up, they just continued shouting at each other as if there was no difference between dream and reality whatsoever.

'How long, Brov?'

But Fergal didn't move. He just stared at The Lamp of the World, as if hypnotized by the blue light.

Filly looked over his shoulder at the watch. 'Eight minutes and fifty-two sec–'

And that's when it happened!

Suddenly, out of nowhere, the kitchen was full of shouting.

'Don't dilly-dally-chop-chop-zip-zip!' cried Filly excitedly. 'Reset the watch, Brov!'

Now they would have to time how long the argument lasted.

Filly made a mental note that it had taken them...what was it again? Oh yes...Eight minutes and fifty-two seconds to start arguing.

BANG!

A noise from the kitchen!

Fergal glanced at Filly nervously.

'Just a chair being knocked over, Brov,' Filly told him in her most soothing voice. (She was an expert in all the possible noises a row could produce.) 'Dad's chair, I believe,' she added.

BANG!

'Mum's chair, Brov.'

Their parents' shadows were moving very fast across the kitchen floor now. They were both shouting at the tops of their voices.

SMASH!

Filly and Fergal flinched.

'Something's been broken, Brov!' cried Filly.

Fergal's frown became even deeper.

To keep him occupied, Filly asked, 'Now, what do you think it could be, Brov?'

'Dunno, Sis.'

'Have a guess, Brov.'

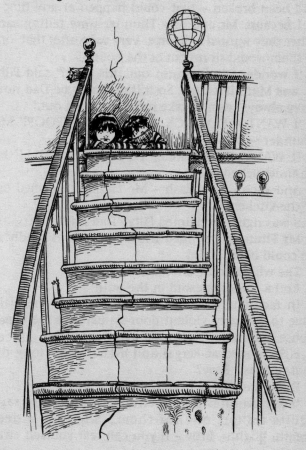

Fergal thought for a while, then suggested, 'Cup, Sis?'

'Don't think so, Brov. You know what I think it was? A teapot. And...there...on the floor by the kitchen door. There's the spout. So I was right! A teapot it was!'

Filly and Fergal knew their parents were in the final stages of the argument now. Not because something had been broken – that could happen at any time – but because Mr and Mrs Thunder were telling each other they wanted a divorce. Very soon after that, one of them would storm out of the house.

'I wonder who'll storm out this time?' said Filly. 'It was Mum last time. So it'll probably be Dad now. They always seem to take turns storming out.'

'I WANT A DIVORCE, YOU NINCOMPOOP!' Mrs Thunder yelled.

'I WANT A DIVORCE, YOU NUMBSKULL!' Mr Thunder yelled back.

And then – in a flash – Mr Thunder stormed out of the kitchen.

'I was right!' exclaimed Filly. 'Dad it is!'

Mr Thunder slammed the front door as loudly as he could behind him.

The whole house shook!

And a crack appeared in the wall!

In fact, there were so many cracks in the walls (due to so many violent door-slams) that the whole house looked like a gigantic jigsaw puzzle.

Filly looked at Fergal and asked, 'How long did that one last, Brov?'

Fergal showed her the watch.

'Four minutes and twenty seconds,' Filly said. 'Quite a short one for them.' She took a deep breath. 'Righto, Brov – if you can tear yourself away from that lamp – we'll record all this information before we forget. And make sure you reset the watch. We've got to time how long it takes for the next argument to start now. Oh, what an interesting hobby this is, Brov!'

They went back to their bedroom and got *The Book of Arguments* from behind the wardrobe.

Filly turned to a new page and this is what she wrote:

DATE
Wednesday 16 August

<u>LENGTH OF TIME BEFORE FIRST ARGUMENT</u>
Eight minutes and fifty-two seconds

<u>LENGTH OF ARGUMENT</u>
Four minutes and twenty seconds

<u>THING (OR THINGS) BROKEN</u>
One teapot

<u>TITLE OF ARGUMENT</u>
The Argument that Broke the Teapot

<u>CAUSE OF ARGUMENT</u>
Not yet known

<u>GENERAL COMMENTS</u>
Flared up very suddenly. Quite loud for a morning argument. No new insults heard. Took place entirely in the kitchen. Two chairs knocked over, but not damaged. Ended with Dad storming out of the house. He slammed the door as usual. Another new crack in the wall.

Once this was done, Filly hid the book again and said, 'Time for the glue!'

After every argument, Filly and Fergal always got a tube of glue and stuck together whatever had been broken. (To be honest, Filly did all the sticking. As for Fergal...well, he just watched.)

Most of their pocket-money (which was hardly anything to begin with) went on glue. Needless to say, with things getting broken every day, a lot of glue was needed. All the tubes (used as well as unused) were kept in the bottom of the wardrobe.

It was through this pile that Fergal was searching now.

'Don't dilly-dally, Brov,' urged Filly. Then added, 'Chop-chop!' for good measure.

Fergal found a new tube of glue and handed it to his sister.

'Righto, Brov,' she said. 'Time to cheer Mum up!'

— 4 —

'Nincompoop!' muttered Mrs Thunder.

She was marching round and round the kitchen table.

Filly and Fergal stood watching in the doorway.

'Nincompoop!' she muttered again, waving her arms in the air.

Mrs Thunder was tall and thin and had long, black hair (which was straggly and full of tangles). She was wearing a bright red dressing-gown that flapped about her like wings, and bright red varnish on all her nails (toes as well as fingers).

'Nincompoop!' she muttered once more. Then added, 'Where's my lipstick?'

After a row, Mrs Thunder put on layer upon layer of bright red lipstick. Her lips were already caked with the stuff, but that didn't stop her taking the tube from her pocket and putting some more on, muttering, 'Nincompoop! Nincompoop!' all the time.

Now, if you're wondering how someone can say 'nincompoop' and put lipstick on without it going all over the place, you'd be right to. It can't be done. Consequently, Mrs Thunder had lipstick on her chin, across her cheeks, and even up her nose.

'Good morning, Mum,' said Filly.

Fergal pulled his jumper up over his eyes.

'My sweethearts!' cried Mrs Thunder. 'You won't believe what that nincompooping father of yours did!'

Now, for some reason, both Mrs Thunder and Mr Thunder were under the impression that their arguments went unheard. As if anyone could fail to hear all that shouting and slamming of doors. But that's what they believed and – rightly or wrongly – Filly never said anything to the contrary.

'What did Dad do, Mum?' asked Filly, picking up the fallen chairs.

'He started an argument!'

'How?'

'He breathed,' snarled Mrs Thunder.

'But Dad has got to breathe,' sighed Filly, collecting the bits of broken teapot together.

'Not necessarily!' snapped Mrs Thunder, smearing lipstick over her lips (and left ear). 'And certainly not the way *he* does it! Sucking the air up through his nose so it makes a whistling noise through his nostril hairs. Ugh!' She shook all over, spitting the 'ugh' out with the ferocity of a gunshot. 'What a disgusting collection of bodily functions that man is!'

Filly had got all the teapot pieces now and was spreading them across the table. She led Fergal over and the two of them sat opposite each other. Filly unscrewed the lid from the glue and started sticking the teapot back together.

'Nincompoop ... nincompoop ... nincompoop ...' Mrs Thunder continued to mutter, still marching

round the kitchen and putting lipstick on. 'You know what your father was put on this planet to do?' she asked Filly.

'Needle you?' suggested Filly.

'That's right! And you know what I've given him?'

'The best years of your life?'

'That's right! And you know what I'm not?'

'A spring chicken?'

'That's right!'

Filly was only right, of course, because she'd heard all this before. After every argument it was always the same complaints, the same grudges, the same moaning.

'Every little thing about your father just needles, needles, needles,' Mrs Thunder was saying, smearing lipstick across her forehead. 'The way his nincompooping hair is falling out – UGH! That flabby nincompooping stomach of his – UGH! UGH! Not to mention his double nincompooping chin – or should I say his *treble* nincompooping chin – UGH! UGH! UGH!' Lipstick was all over her nose now. 'And he's got hair in his ears! Can you believe that? I lie in bed at night and I look into his ears and all I can see is straggly hairs and lumps of wax. UGH! It makes me feel sick! And you know what else needles me?'

'His walk?' offered Filly.

'His *nincompooping* walk! And his nincompooping voice! That needles me too. And the nincompooping way he eats! And then – after he's eaten – his stomach makes all those disgusting nincompooping gurgling noises – UGHHHH!'

Sometimes it took ages for Mrs Thunder to calm down after an argument. Her nincompooping and lipsticking could go on indefinitely (sometimes leading straight into the next argument) unless Filly did something to calm her down.

And there was only one thing that would do it.

'Honeymoon!' exclaimed Filly, sticking one piece of broken teapot to another.

Mrs Thunder looked at Filly. 'Honeymoon?' she said.

'Right, Mum! Why don't you tell us about your honeymoon?'

Mrs Thunder was suddenly much calmer. Slowly, she put the lipstick back in her pocket and sat at the kitchen table.

'Oh, my honeymoon, my sweethearts,' she sighed, smiling at the memories. 'How can I describe my honeymoon! It was so...so...gorrrjusss!'

Fergal's eyes reappeared above the neck of his jumper.

'What did Dad look like in those days?' asked Filly.

'Gorrrjusss!' beamed Mrs Thunder, her eyes twinkling. 'He had a black quiff and lots of muscles. Every time I looked at him I felt things go fizz and pop inside me. And you know how my heart went?'

'Pitty-pat?' suggested Filly. (Again she knew all the answers because she'd heard it all before.)

'That's right!' said Mrs Thunder. '*So* pitty-pat, in fact, that we got married just two weeks after we first met. And then...then our honeymoon!'

'Where did you go?'

'To an island.'

'What was it like?'

'Gorrrjusss!' declared Mrs Thunder. 'There was golden sunshine every day. Not a cloud in the perfect blue sky.' Mrs Thunder gazed above as if she could still see this perfect sky and not a cracked ceiling and sixty-watt light-bulb.

'And what about the beaches?' asked Filly. 'I bet they were gorgeous too.'

'Totally and utterly gorrrjusss!' Mrs Thunder told her. 'Nothing but yellow sand for as far as the eye could see.' And, again, she gazed round her as if seeing this perfect shoreline and not cracked walls and crockery. 'The sunshine made the sand so hot,' she continued dreamily. 'Like walking on hot coals.'

'Did you get burnt at all?'

'I did, my sweetheart. I was running across the beach one day when, all of a sudden, one of my shoes – or, rather, one of my flip-flops – came off. I got a blister on my little toe. And your dad – oh, it was so thrilling – your dad took my tiny foot in his huge hands and he blew on my blister until all the stinging had gone.'

'He made you a heart too, didn't he, Mum?'

'That's right, my sweetheart! He made me a big heart out of seashells. And in the middle he wrote MR THUNDER LOVES MRS THUNDER. Oh, it was so romantic. I made him a heart in return. And in the middle of mine I wrote ... guess what?'

'MRS THUNDER LOVES MR THUNDER?'

'That's right! Oh, it was all so...so...gorrrjusss! And the birds!' Mrs Thunder was getting quite excited now. 'The birds were all different colours. Gorrrjusss, gorrrjusss, gorrrjusss!'

'Tell us about the sea,' Filly urged. 'We want to hear about that. Don't we, Brov?'

Fergal blinked. 'Yep, Sis.'

'Oh, my sweethearts.' Mrs Thunder ruffled Fergal's hair. 'The sea was gorrrjusss too. It was as blue as the sky and so clear you could see right to the bottom.'

'And you could see a shipwreck, I suppose?'

'That's right! One day your dad and I went out on a row-boat. And we looked over the side and there – on the bottom of the sea – we saw a shipwreck. The boat was hundreds of years old. Made of wood with tall masts. We were going to dive down and explore it...but we couldn't.'

'Why, Mum?' asked Filly.

'Because there were tiny red fish in the water,' Mrs Thunder explained. 'And these fish were covered in poisonous needles. If you got pricked by one of them you got very sick. So your dad and I just stayed in the boat and looked at the wreck from a distance. Shame really. After all, I'm too old for that sort of thing now.' She sighed. 'Exploring shipwrecks is for when you're young.'

'But you're not old now!' insisted Filly.

'Thank you, my sweetheart,' said Mrs Thunder. 'But I'm no spring chicken either.' And a sad look came into her eyes.

Filly tried to lighten the mood again. 'There were beautiful dolphins in the sea as well, weren't there, Mum?' she asked. The main part of the teapot was back together now. All that remained was to stick on the spout, and glue the two halves of the lid together.

'Plenty of dolphins,' Mrs Thunder replied, the melancholy going from her eyes. 'They would jump in the air and do somersaults.'

'What clothes did you wear?'

'Oh, my sweethearts,' breathed Mrs Thunder, looking at them both. 'They were gorrrjusss. We wore things called Hawaiian shirts and Bermuda shorts. They were covered in pictures of volcanoes and palm trees and frothy waves. And...and we wore sunglasses to keep the sun out of our eyes and – as I've already said – flip-flops to stop us burning our feet.'

'I bet you looked totally gorgeous, Mum,' Filly told her. 'Right, Brov?'

'Yep, Sis,' agreed Fergal, staring at his mother.

'I *was* gorrrjusss!' confirmed Mrs Thunder. 'I had a suntan and a twenty-two-inch waist.' And she ran her hands over her body, as if feeling the perfect skin and body of the past and not the pasty scragginess of the present.

'What sort of things did you eat?' Filly had just finished attaching the spout to the main body of the teapot and now she was starting to glue the lid back together.

'We ate gorrrjusss things!' Mrs Thunder licked her lips (getting lipstick all over her tongue). 'There were palm trees, you see, and your dad would climb

up and shake down a coconut to eat. Oh, my sweethearts...look at me!' Mrs Thunder's eyes were brimming with tears. 'The waterworks are off just thinking about it.' She took a tissue from her pocket and dabbed her eyes.

'You loved Dad then, didn't you, Mum?'

'That's right, my sweetheart.'

'And he loved you?'

'That's right.'

'And you still love him?'

'Well...I suppose so.'

'And he still loves you?'

'I suppose so.'

'So you still love each other?'

Mrs Thunder thought for a while. 'I suppose you must be right,' she said at last. 'We still love each other.'

'Teapot mended!' announced Filly.

'Look at that!' exclaimed Mrs Thunder, clapping her hands together. 'You're so clever with that glue, my sweetheart.' She kissed Filly. 'And you,' she continued, kissing Fergal, 'are so clever for just sitting there and blinking at me with those big eyes of yours.'

Filly could see Fergal smile beneath his jumper.

'Go and find your dad,' said Mrs Thunder, getting to her feet. 'Tell him he can breathe all he wants. In fact, he can breathe through his hairy ears for all I care!'

'Righto, Mum.' Filly grabbed hold of Fergal's hand. 'Don't dilly-dally, Brov!' They made their way to the front door. 'Time to cheer Dad up now,' whispered Filly. 'What an interesting hobby this is!'

Now, most streets are full of houses and have cars driving up and down them (or parked along the kerbs). If you live in a street, I bet it looks pretty much like this. Perhaps there's a corner shop and a letter-box somewhere and people to say 'good morning' or 'good night' to (depending on the time of day).

But Filly and Fergal's street wasn't like that.

To be honest, when they left their front door they didn't see anything that looked like a street at all.

It looked more like...well, I'll tell you what Filly thought it looked like.

The surface of the Moon, that's what.

Let me explain why.

Most of the other houses had been knocked down. Those that weren't totally demolished were half demolished. And those that weren't half demolished were waiting to be demolished, their windows and doors boarded up with wood or corrugated iron.

The houses were being knocked down by a large
crane that swung an enormous ball and chain
through the air. The ball hit a wall and –
CRASH!
A wall would fall down!
Then the crane would swing the ball again and –
CRASH!
Another wall would fall down!
And the crane would keep doing this until all that
was left of the house was a pile of rubble.
The only house that was both still standing and
had people in it was the house where Filly and
Fergal lived. But they knew that pretty soon – like
everyone else – they'd be moving.
All they were waiting for was a letter.
'One day,' Mrs Thunder kept on telling them, 'we'll
get a letter from The Powers that Be. And then we'll
have a brand-new house with a garden. And we'll
have neighbours again. Won't that be gorrrjusss?'

But Filly wasn't so sure.

After all, neighbours had ears. Ears that would hear Mr And Mrs Thunder shouting and breaking things. And the neighbours would talk. And, before long, everyone would know.

Perhaps it's best to stay where we are, Filly thought. On The Surface of the Moon.

Filly had called it that ever since she'd seen a television documentary about the first manned Moon landing. (That was in the days when they still had a television, of course. 'The Argument that Broke the Television' had occurred nearly nine months ago, and a new one had never been bought.) Filly had been struck by how similar the surface of the Moon looked to her own neighbourhood. Only here, instead of Moon-mountains, there were half-demolished buildings: and, instead of Moon-craters, there were big holes where buildings once stood: and, instead of Moon-boulders, there were lumps of concrete.

Filly had pointed out the similarity to Fergal and he'd said, 'Yep, Sis,' a little more enthusiastically than usual, so she knew the idea appealed to him.

Filly could see the crane swinging its ball and chain in the distance. It looked like a dinosaur against the grey sky. They heard the thud of a building falling far away.

Then they heard a voice.

'Numbskull!' it muttered.

It was their dad!

'Numbskull!' it muttered again.

Hand in hand, Filly and Fergal walked towards the sound of the voice. They climbed over a pile of rubble and...there was Mr Thunder, marching round and round a pile of bricks.

He was small and plump, had black hair (with a bald spot at the back), and was wearing a bright green dressing-gown that flapped in the breeze.

'Numbskull!' he muttered once more. Then added, 'Where's my comb?'

After every row, Mr Thunder would try to comb his hair over his bald spot.

'Good morning, Dad,' said Filly, approaching him.

Fergal pulled his jumper up over his eyes.

'My kiddywinks!' cried Mr Thunder, taking the comb from his dressing-gown pocket. 'You won't believe what that numbskull mother of yours did!'

'What did Mum do, Dad?' asked Filly.

'She started an argument!'

'How?'

'She looked at me,' Mr Thunder snarled.

'But Mum has to look at you now and then,' sighed Filly.

'Not necessarily!' Mr Thunder snapped, combing his hair vigorously and smoothing it flat over his bald spot. 'And certainly not the way *she* does it! Her eyes are all watery and bloodshot – UGH!' He shook all over, then continued. 'You know what your mother was put on this planet to do?'

'Needle you?' suggested Filly.

'Right you are! And you know what I've given her?'

'The best years of your life?'

'Right you are! And you know what I'm not?'

'A spring chicken?'

'Right you are!' Mr Thunder continued marching round and round the pile of rubble. Every time he combed his hair over the bald spot a breeze blew it off, so he had to do it all over again. 'Every little thing about her just needles, needles, needles,' he moaned. 'The way she has bits of food stuck between her numbskull teeth – UGH! The way she has lumps of sleep stuck to her numbskull eyes – UGH! UGH! The way her flabby stomach wobbles when she walks – UGH! UGH! UGH!'

It's about time I put a stop to this, thought Filly.

'Honeymoon!' she exclaimed

Mr Thunder stood very still and stared at Filly. 'Honeymoon?' he said.

'Right, Dad! Why don't you tell us about your honeymoon?'

Mr Thunder was suddenly much calmer. Slowly, he put his comb back in his pocket and sat on a slab of concrete.

'Oh, my honeymoon, my kiddywinks,' he sighed, smiling at the memories. 'How can I describe it? It was...wunnerful!'

Fergal's eyes reappeared above the neck of his jumper.

'What did Mum look like in those days?' Filly asked.

'Wunnerful!' exclaimed Mr Thunder, his eyes twinkling. 'She had long, wavy hair and a waist so slim I could wrap my arm right round it. My whole body went ping and zap when I was near her. And you know how my heart went?'

'Boom-boom?'

'Right you are!' Mr Thunder touched his chest as if feeling that long-distant booming.

'Tell us about the honeymoon nights, Dad,' urged Filly. 'Mum has already told us about the days.'

'She has!' exclaimed Mr Thunder. 'She's told you about the blue sky and the clear blue sea?'

'Right!' Filly assured him. 'Right, Brov?'

'Yep, Sis,' agreed Fergal.

'And the shipwreck?'

'Right! Right, Brov?'

'Yep, Sis.'

'And the beaches?'

'Right! Right, Brov?'

'Yep, Sis.'

'The blister?'

'Right! Right, Brov?'

'Yep, Sis.'

'And the coconuts and the seashell hearts and the birds and the dolphins and the – '

'She's told us, Dad!' interrupted Filly. 'All we need to know about are the nights. Now, why don't you begin with...the sunsets.'

'The sunsets!' Mr Thunder's eyes grew wide with wonder. 'Oh, they were so wunnerful, my kiddywinks. Your mum and I would stand on the beach and watch the sun go down just for the joy of it. All those reds and yellows and oranges and scarlets and mauves. Like a painting, it was.' And he gazed above as if he could still see this dazzling sky, and not the endless grey clouds. 'Wunnerful!' he sighed. 'Just wunnerful!'

'I bet there were shooting stars.'

'Right you are! Blazing across the sky like –'

'Like the biggest fireworks in The Whole History of Fireworks!' Filly finished for him.

Mr Thunder smiled and nodded. 'Oh yes, everything was wunnerful on the island. No wonder the volcano never erupted.'

'The...vol...volcano?' stammered Filly. (She'd never heard any mention of a volcano before. Even Fergal blinked a few times with surprise.)

Mr Thunder nodded. 'The volcano in the middle of the island,' he told them.

'But...but...' Filly took a few deep breaths to calm herself. 'Was it big?'

'Very big.'

'And was it...well, alive?'

'Very much so. You could see black smoke coming from the top.'

'Then why didn't it explode?'

'I'll tell you,' said Mr Thunder, getting a little more comfortable on his concrete slab. He pulled Filly towards him and sat her on his right knee, then sat Fergal on his left. 'You see, the people that went to the island were people like your mum and I. We were all – '

'Honeymooners?' interrupted Filly.

'Some of them, yes. But what I meant was we were all on holiday. None of us actually lived there. And, of course, everyone thought the island was wunnerful. So wunnerful that no one ever wanted to go home – '

'That doesn't explain why the volcano never exploded,' insisted Filly. 'Does it, Brov?'

'Nope, Sis.'

'I'm getting to that, my kiddywinks,' explained Mr Thunder. 'You see, there was a legend about the island. And this legend said that the volcano would only erupt when somebody actually *wanted* to leave the island. The day that somebody said, "I want to go home," then – BAHM!'

Filly and Fergal jumped.

'But...but that would be terrible!' gasped Filly. 'All those beautiful beaches and palm trees would be destroyed. And what about all the birds and...and the dolphins and...and – '

'Now, don't get all worked up, my kiddywink.' Mr Thunder gently squeezed Filly's hand. 'The island is so totally and utterly wunnerful I don't think anyone will ever want to leave.'

'You left!' Filly reminded him.

'I know I did. But... I didn't want to.' His voice became very sad. 'Sometimes it seems to me that my whole life changed the day I left that island. One day I had a quiff and was covered in muscles and surrounded by golden sand and blue sky, and the next day I was surrounded by...' He looked at the rubble and grey skies and couldn't even bring himself to finish.

'By me and Fergal!' Filly finished for him. 'You're surrounded by us!'

'Right you are!' agreed Mr Thunder, smiling. 'So it

was worth leaving the island after all!' And he kissed them both.

If only it was always like this, thought Filly. Fergal looks so happy inside his jumper now. It reminds me of the days when Mum and Dad used to laugh and hug and call each other 'my love' – Love! Crikey! I haven't got Dad to say that he and Mum still love each other yet. All that talk of the volcano distracted me! Mustn't dilly-dally! Here goes –

'Dad,' said Filly, 'you loved Mum when you were on the island, didn't you?'

'Right you are, my kiddywink!'

'And she loved you?'

'Right you are!'

'And you still love her?'

'Well ... I suppose so.'

'And she still loves you?'

'I suppose so.'

'So you still love each other?'

Mr Thunder thought for a while. 'I suppose you must be right,' he said. 'We still love each other.' He jumped to his feet so fast that Filly and Fergal almost fell to the ground. 'I'm going back to your mum!' he said. 'She can look at me all she wants.' And he rushed across the rubble towards their house.

'Another success, Brov,' commented Filly. 'Wonder how long it will take them to start arguing again. How long's it been so far?'

Fergal took the stop-watch from his pocket and showed it to Filly.

'One hour and twenty-two minutes and fifteen seconds,' she noted. 'Righto! Let's go back and have some breakfast.' They started to walk home. 'You hungry, Brov?'

'Yep, Sis.'

'I'm starving. My stomach keeps making all those strange gurgling noises Mum hates so much. Come on now! Don't dilly-dally! Chop-chop! Zip–'

Filly never finished the second 'zip'.

Because she'd just seen something very surprising.

So surprising, in fact, that she stopped walking as well as talking.

— 6 —

Now (as I've said before) Filly and Fergal rarely saw any other people on The Surface of the Moon. So to see anyone would be a surprise. But the person they'd just seen was particularly surprising.

It was a very, very, very old woman, and – although the day was far from cold – she was wearing at least five overcoats. All the coats were dirty and full of holes, as were her stockings and – wait for it – her wellington boots. Yes, wellington boots! Even though it was the middle of August and not raining at all. The old woman was also wearing a very long scarf and woollen mittens, and carrying seven plastic bags full of heaven knows what.

But the most surprising thing was the woman's hair.

Because it appeared to be ... wood!

Twigs were all over her scalp and some of them still had leaves on.

The woman was walking round and round in circles, obviously looking for something in the rubble. 'Where can they be?' she was muttering. 'Where?'

'Have you lost something?' asked Filly, recovering from her surprise.

The old woman jumped. 'Oh, you startled me!' she gasped, looking at Filly. Her eyes were very small and very blue, like chips of summer sky. 'Now be careful where you step, my chicklings. You might tread right on them.'

'On what?' Filly wanted to know.

'My false teeth!'

'Your false teeth!'

'And they're such lovely choppers too,' the old woman went on. 'Very white and sparkling. I feel

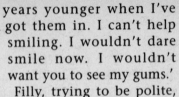

years younger when I've got them in. I can't help smiling. I wouldn't dare smile now. I wouldn't want you to see my gums.'

Filly, trying to be polite, remarked, 'I wouldn't mind seeing your gums.'

'A young chickling like you doesn't want to see a withered chickling's gums. Oh no. Now, where can my choppers be? I hope I haven't lost them. It was the luckiest day of my life when I found them.'

'You *found* them!' exclaimed Filly.

'I did, my chickling.'

'But...where?'

'In the rubble somewhere. They were just lying there in the dirt, smiling at me. So I picked them up and popped them into my mouth. And – tra-la! – I could smile again. Only problem is ... well, the teeth are too big for me, so they keep popping out of my mouth.

'Only yesterday I was begging for some money and – just as this someone was about to give me a few coins – I said, "Thank you," and – would you believe it? – out shot my choppers! Hit the someone right between the eyes. I said, "Sorry," so many times I lost count. But still the someone refused to give me any money. Which wasn't fair, I felt. After all, wasn't as if I meant to whack them with my choppers.

'Now, are you two chicklings going to help me look? Your young chicklings' eyes can see a lot better than my old chickling's eyes.'

Carefully, Filly and Fergal started searching.

They'd only been looking a couple of minutes when Fergal said, 'Here, Sis,' and pointed at something.

'My choppers!' cried the old woman, picking them up. 'Now I'll just give them a little dusting on my coat...There we are! And now...in they go!' She slipped the teeth into her mouth, jiggled them into place with her tongue, then smiled broadly. 'Tra-la! How do I look?'

The dentures were obviously much too big for her, and there were still bits of dirt stuck to them, but Filly said they looked fine and Fergal chipped in with, 'Yep, Sis.'

'Now I'm ready to face the world,' announced the old woman, finding it a little difficult to talk through such massive teeth. 'Let me introduce myself. My name is Juno Whisper. Chicklings of my own ancient years call me Juno, but younger chicklings – like yourselves – usually call me Miss Whisper.'

'Nice to meet you, Miss Whisper,' Filly said. 'My name is Filly and this is my brother, Fergal.'

'And what a lovely couple of chicklings you are!' Miss Whisper noticed Fergal staring at the top of her head. 'What are you looking at with those big dark eyes, my chickling?'

Fergal blinked, but didn't answer.

Filly explained for him. 'To be honest, I think it's your hair. Is it...Oh, I'm sure this is going to sound very rude.'

'Just spit it out,' Miss Whisper told her. 'I'll allow you one rude question for helping me find my teeth.'

Filly took a deep breath. 'Your hair...' she began. Another breath. 'Well, it looks like...wood.'

'That's because it *is* wood, my chicklings,' Miss

Whisper said casually. 'I lost all my real hair years ago. What you see on my head now is a wig. Well, when I say wig, what I really mean is...a nest!'

'A *nest*!' gasped Filly.

'Let me explain, my chicklings. Not so long ago I found this nest in some rubble and I was immediately struck by how easily it would fit on my head. So I put it on and – tra-la! – I had hair. Now, I know it still looks a little wooden, but wooden hair is better than no hair at all, wouldn't you agree?'

Filly and Fergal nodded, too surprised to talk for the moment.

'And it cost me no money at all,' Miss Whisper went on. 'I can't believe all those famous film stars pay fortunes for wigs when they can just as easily put a bird's nest on their head. What's that noise?'

'I'm afraid it's my stomach,' Filly explained, more than a little embarrassed.

'Your stomach! But haven't you had your breakfast yet?'

Filly shook her head.

'But...is that where you live, over there?' Miss Whisper pointed at their house.

Filly nodded.

'I saw a man rush into that house a little while ago. Was that your dad?'

Again Filly nodded.

'And I noticed a woman peering from behind the kitchen curtains. That was your mum, I suppose?'

More nodding.

'But if you've got a mum and a dad, why haven't they given you any – WHOOPS! There go my choppers!' Miss Whisper's teeth shot out of her mouth.

They whizzed through the air.

Filly caught the top set.

And Fergal caught the bottom.

'What clever chicklings!' declared Miss Whisper. She put her teeth back in. 'Now, where were we? Oh yes. No breakfast. Why, my chicklings, why?'

'Well...' began Filly.

'Yes?' coaxed Miss Whisper. 'Don't be shy.'

'Mum and Dad argue quite a lot, you see, and –'

'But that's monstrous! What naughty grown-up chicklings they are. And with a couple of adorable little chicklings like you to look after as well. Absolutely monstrous!'

'Oh, it's not too bad,' insisted Filly.

Miss Whisper looked dubious. 'It's not?'

'No. We've made it our hobby. And it really is very interesting. Right, Brov?'

'Yep, Sis,' agreed Fergal flatly.

'Is that really so, my little chickling?' Miss Whisper looked directly at Fergal.

He blinked, but did not answer.

'My brother only talks to me,' Filly explained. 'He doesn't even talk to Mum and Dad.'

'I see,' said Miss Whisper thoughtfully. 'So tell me more about your hobby.'

'Well... we've got this book called *The Book of Arguments*. And we've got a stop-watch – Show Miss Whisper the stop-watch, Brov.'

Fergal did as he was asked.

'And we time all the arguments...' Filly went on to explain everything.

But she could tell Miss Whisper knew the truth. She could see it in the old woman's eyes. Miss Whisper knew it wasn't interesting at all, and that Filly was only doing it to keep Fergal's mind off things.

'Well, I'm sure you're right,' said Miss Whisper

when Filly had finished. 'But sometimes – hobby or no hobby – listening to grown-up chicklings shouting can really get on top of little chicklings. So, if things should ever get on top of you – not that they will, because, as you say, it's a very interesting hobby, but *if* they should – then I've got something that might just help. Now where is it?' She started rummaging through her plastic bags. 'It's here somewhere, I'm sure it is,' she muttered. 'I saw it just the other day.' She pulled out a broken lampshade. 'No, not this.' Then a bowler hat. 'Not this.' Then an empty beer bottle. 'Certainly not this...Ah, here it is! Tra-la!'

With a great flourish, Miss Whisper held something in the air.

It was in the shape of a very large spoon. Only, it seemed to be made of...well, rock! It was dark brown and covered in lumps and bumps.

'Wh-what is it?' asked Filly.

'This, my chickling,' came the reply, 'is the meteorite spoon!'

'The meteorite spoon!' gasped Filly.

Miss Whisper nodded.

'But...how? Why?' Filly's mind was so full of questions, she didn't know where to begin.

'Let me explain, my chicklings.' Miss Whisper took a deep breath, repositioned the dentures on her gums, then began. 'A long time ago, when I was a young chickling and didn't have to wear a bird's nest on my head or someone else's teeth in my mouth, I lived in a house. Oh, I know what you're thinking – She's nothing but an old bag lady. How could she ever have had a house? But what I am now is not what I always was. Oh no. And once I had a house and it was lovely. I was the happiest chickling in all the world in those days.'

'So what happened?' asked Filly.

'That's what I'm getting to.' Miss Whisper took another deep breath. 'One night I was fast asleep in bed when, all of a sudden, I heard the strangest noise ever. Wooosh! it went. Wooo – Oh, there go my choppers!'

And, once again, the teeth shot out of her mouth.

This time Filly caught the bottom set.

And Fergal caught the top.

'You're getting dab hands at the old chopper catching, my chicklings,' remarked Miss Whisper, putting them back in her mouth. 'They should make it an Olympic sport. You two would get gold medals every time. Now then...where was I?'

'Wooosh!' Filly reminded her.

'Right!' Miss Whisper collected her thoughts. 'I was lying in bed and I heard woo – well, I won't do

it again in
case my teeth
fly out. They
might knock you
out next time, and
that wouldn't do at all.
Perhaps you'd do the
noise for me, just to help
me get in the mood.'

'Wooosh!' went Filly.

'I jumped out of bed.'

'Wooosh!'

'I looked all round the
house.'

'Wooosh!'

'I thought it might be a gas leak.
But, no! The sound was coming
from outside the house. I rushed
out! The sound got louder!'

'Wooosh!' went Filly, a
little louder.

'Much louder than that!'

'Wooooosh!' went Filly.

And this time another
voice joined in.

It was Fergal!

Filly looked at him in surprise. He was actually
helping her with the 'wooshing'. His eyes were
wider than she had ever seen them before.

'I looked up,' Miss Whisper continued, 'and I saw
it! In the night sky! Bright and red! It was a meteor!'

'Wooooosh!' went Filly and Fergal.

'A meteor heading straight for my house!'

'Wooooossshhh!'

'I ran as fast as I could!'

WOOOOOOSSSSSHHHH!

— 55 —

'Woooooooossssshhhhh!'
'And then –'
'WOOOOOOOOSSSSSSHHHHH!'
'CRASH! The meteor hit my house! My lovely house was destroyed before my very eyes. Nothing left, my chicklings. No bed, no television, no chairs, no crockery. Nothing. Just a big smouldering crater.' Miss Whisper sighed sadly. 'When everything had cooled down I went to have a look. Oh, what a mess it was. My lovely home all gone in one woooshing moment –' Her teeth nearly popped out then, but

she caught them just in time and pushed them back
in without batting an eyelid. 'And all I could find to
remind me of the home I once had was...this!' She
held the meteorite spoon in the air. 'Some of the
molten metal from the meteor must have covered a
kitchen spoon. And this is it! I've kept it on me all
these long years. And now...now I'm giving it to
you, my very special chicklings.'

'But...why?' asked Filly.

'Because it might help you.' Miss Whisper smiled.
'I know you've made a hobby of your parents'

arguing, and it must be interesting, but – as I've already said – sometimes things get on top of little chicklings and make them want to scream. Am I right?'

Slowly, Fergal nodded.

'Well, when that happens...just dig a hole with the meteorite spoon and scream into it. Scream for as long and as loud as you want. And afterwards – tra-la! – things will be a lot better, I promise you.' She handed the spoon to Fergal.

He took it as if it were precious treasure.

Suddenly...shouting filled the air!

'That's Mum and Dad!' cried Filly. 'How long between arguments, Brov? Chop-chop! The stop-watch!'

Fergal showed her the watch.

'Two hours exactly!' Filly noted. 'Now, reset the watch, Brov. We've got to time this argument.' She looked at Miss Whisper. 'We'd like to stay and talk, Miss Whisper, but I'm afraid we really must get back to the house as zip-zip as possible.'

'I understand, my chicklings. Your hobby calls.' Miss Whisper picked up her bags and started walking away. 'It's been lovely meeting you both,' she said, smiling.

'Lovely meeting you too,' said Filly, grabbing Fergal's hand and rushing towards the house.

'You should get something to eat,' Miss Whisper called over her shoulder.

'Righto! And thank you –'

BANG! went something in the house.

Filly said, 'Now, I don't think that was anything actually breaking, Brov! Oh, please be more chop-chop!'

But Fergal was dragging his heels, looking back at

Miss Whisper as she walked off into the distance.

Just as they reached the front door, Fergal pulled his hand from Filly's grasp and waved at the old woman. 'Goodbye, Miss!' he shouted.

Miss Whisper was a long way away now. Fergal could barely see her waving back. But he could hear her.

'Be brave, my chicklings,' she called, 'be brave!'

—8—

That afternoon (after the second argument of the day was over and their parents had been 'honeymooned' back together again) Filly and Fergal sat in their room and brought *The Book of Arguments* up to date. Or rather, Filly did. Fergal just sat on his bed and blinked at the meteorite spoon.

'Righto!' said Filly briskly. 'The first thing we've got to do is enter the cause of today's first argument. Right, Brov?'

'Yep, Sis,' Fergal responded absently.

'Now, Mum says it was because Dad was breathing. And Dad says it was because Mum was looking at him. But I suspect Mum was only looking at Dad because his breathing was annoying her. So I'll just put "Dad breathing" as the cause. You in agreement with that, Brov?'

Another absent, 'Yep, Sis.'

Filly wrote it in the book.

'And now on to today's second argument,' Filly continued. 'Now, nothing was actually broken in this argument, which means we save on the glue, Brov. But a lot of food was thrown about. The house was a terrible mess. There were baked beans everywhere and even some rashers of bacon stuck to the ceiling. So, again if you're in agreement, Brov, I think we should call this "The Argument that Broke the Food".' Filly smiled at her own inventiveness. 'How do you like that, Brov?'

'Fine, Sis.'

'Just fine?' complained Filly. 'Oh really, Brov, I do

wish you'd give credit where credit's due.'

But Fergal just continued staring at the spoon.

Filly sighed and wrote:

TIME BETWEEN ARGUMENTS
Two hours

LENGTH OF SECOND ARGUMENT
Five hours and eight minutes and twelve seconds

THING (OR THINGS) BROKEN
Lots of food

TITLE OF ARGUMENT
The Argument that Broke the Food

CAUSE OF ARGUMENT
Dad yawned and Mum saw all his fillings and said, 'UGH!'

GENERAL COMMENTS
We weren't in the house when this one started, but we rushed back as soon as we heard it. There was food flying everywhere. I got a pickled herring in my face and Fergal got some frozen peas down the back of his jumper. Ended with Mum storming out of the house and slamming the door. Another huge crack in the wall. This argument was very noisy.

But if Filly thought *that* argument was loud, it was nothing – repeat: nothing – compared to what would take place later that evening.

After Mr and Mrs Thunder had cleaned up the house (unsticking the bacon from the ceiling proved particularly tricky), it was time to have something to eat.

Now – don't forget – most of the food had been ruined.

In fact, there were only four eggs left.

Filly, afraid this might trigger another row, insisted, 'Yummy! I could just do with a boiled egg! I wouldn't eat steak and chips if you put it in front of me. Right, Brov?'

'Yep, Sis.'

(Although, of course, steak and chips is exactly what they wanted. Having not eaten all day, they were starving and their stomachs were rumbling like crazy.)

Mrs Thunder boiled the eggs and they all sat around the table to eat.

Now, meal-times were the tensest times of all in the Thunder household. With Mr and Mrs Thunder sitting opposite each other, and with Mr Thunder disgusted by the sight of Mrs Thunder's eyes, and Mrs Thunder disgusted by the sound of Mr Thunder breathing, there was ample opportunity for a real humdinger of a quarrel.

But, as it turned out, the argument wasn't caused by bloodshot eyes or whistling nostrils.

It was caused by the way Mr Thunder took the top off his boiled egg.

You see, while Mrs Thunder sliced the top off hers with a knife, Mr Thunder gradually chipped his away with a teaspoon.

Tap-tap-tap! went the spoon.

Filly could see it was annoying her mother.

Tap-tap-tap-tap!

Filly glanced at Fergal.

He was eating his egg and staring at the meteorite spoon in his lap, so he was unaware of the imminent explosion...

TAP! TAP! TAP!

Tap-tap-tap-tap-tap!

Mrs Thunder clenched her teeth.

Tap-tap-tap-tap-tap-tap!

Mrs Thunder's temples throbbed.

Tap-tap-tap-tap-tap-tap-tap!

'Must you!' barked Mrs Thunder at last.

'Must I what?' asked Mr Thunder, baffled.

'Tap away at that nincompooping egg of yours!' she hissed. 'It's taking you a lifetime and a half! Why can't you just slice off the top like the rest of humanity? That's the proper way to eat an egg!'

TAP! TAP!

'There *is* no proper way!' responded Mr Thunder, jumping to his feet. 'Besides, you're such a vacuum cleaner in the eats department I don't know why you don't just shove the whole egg into that mouth of yours and gulp it down in one go, shell and all!'

TAP!

Mrs Thunder got to her feet now.

'The stop-watch, Brov!' Filly whispered urgently. 'Don't dilly-dally! They've started –'

And then she saw that something was wrong with Fergal.

He was trembling all over. And there were tears in his eyes.

Oh no! thought Filly. He's going to start crying again! I knew it was all getting too much for him.

'Don't worry, Brov.' Filly patted his hand. 'It's our hobby! That's all! Buck up –'

But it wasn't working!

Tears were rolling into the neck of his jumper. And he was clutching the meteorite spoon so tightly his knuckles were white.

Mrs Thunder threw her egg at Mr Thunder.

It hit him right on his bald spot!

Mr Thunder threw his egg at Mrs Thunder.

It got stuck in her straggly hair!

'You're a mound of blackheads inside a sweaty vest!' yelled Mrs Thunder.

'You're a tatty dressing-gown with wrinkles inside!' yelled Mr Thunder.

'You're a pile of fat with a bald spot!'

'You're a lump of gristle with lipstick on!'

Fergal rushed out of the room.

Filly followed him into the hallway.

'Don't let it get to you, Brov!' she urged him.
'Buck up! Chop-chop! Zip –'
CRASH!
The table had been knocked over!
'Don't worry, Brov!'
SMMMAAASSSHHH!
Breaking plates!
Fergal trembled even more.
'Don't worry, Bro –'
Mr Thunder stormed into the hallway.

Mrs Thunder chased after him.
'And where do you think you're going?'
demanded Mrs Thunder of Mr Thunder.
'Upstairs to pack a suitcase,' Mr Thunder told her.
'I'M LEAVING YOU!'
Leaving! thought Filly. No one has ever said
they'd actually leave before! Dad is leaving! He's
going to pack a suitcase! Oh no! Please don't leave!
'*You're* not leaving!' cried Mrs Thunder. '*I'M*
LEAVING!' She started to push past him. 'Out of my

way! I want to pack my suitcase first!'

They both tried to push past each other, each one trying to get upstairs first.

'Get your bloodshot eyes away from me!' roared Mr Thunder.

'Get your dandruffy hair away from me!' roared Mrs Thunder.

'Mum!' cried Filly. 'Dad! Stop!'

But they were too busy pushing and insulting each other to hear.

They can't leave! thought Filly. They can't!

Fergal was trembling more and more.

Mr and Mrs Thunder reached the top of the stairs, still trying to push past each other.

Filly saw what was about to happen a moment before it occurred.

'The Lamp!' she cried.

But it was too late!

Mr and Mrs Thunder had knocked The Lamp of the World over.

It started to roll down the stairs.

No! thought Filly. Don't break! It's Mum and Dad's favourite thing! Please don't break!

Mr and Mrs Thunder watched it roll down the stairs.

'The Lamp!' cried Mrs Thunder.

'The Lamp!' cried Mr Thunder.

Every time the Lamp hit a step the whole family flinched.

Don't break! thought Filly.

Another step!

Flinch!

Don't break!

Another step!

Flinch!

Don't break!

And then...
It bounced off the final step...
Rolled across the floor...
And hit – oh, so gently – first Filly's big black boots and then Fergal's.
And...
Broke clean in half!

Crikey! thought Filly. It's 'The Argument that Broke the World'!

She looked up at Mr and Mrs Thunder.

They were staring in horror at the broken Lamp.

'You did that!' snarled Mrs Thunder, pointing at Filly.

'M-me?' stammered Filly.

'That's right! You kicked it with those clumpy boots of yours!'

'But I didn't, Mum! Honestly!'

'Don't argue with me, you stretched zebra!'

'And you did it too!' snarled Mr Thunder, pointing at Fergal. 'You kicked it with your boots as well, you squashed-in-your-jumper excuse of a boy!'

And that's when Fergal ran!

He ran to the door under the stairs, yanked it open and scarpered down to the cellar.

'Now look what you've done!' hollered Filly at her parents. 'I don't know why you take it out on us! It was *you* who knocked the Lamp over –'

But Mrs Thunder had heard Mr Thunder's breath, and Mr Thunder had seen Mrs Thunder's eyes, so they were already arguing again every bit as ferociously as before.

Filly rushed after Fergal.

The cellar was lit by a single light-bulb. There were a few cardboard boxes scattered around and a rusty old bike that Filly used to play on (when there were streets and pavements to ride on outside, that is).

Fergal was huddled in a corner. He was clutching the meteorite spoon and crying so hard he could barely breathe. 'Wah-wah-wah!' he went.

'Oh, Brov,' sighed Filly, going to him. 'Don't cry! Please don't cry!'

'Wah-wah-wah!'

'Mum and Dad didn't mean it,' Filly assured him. 'You know how they get when they're needled by each other. They say things they don't mean. They'll say they're sorry later. You're not squashed into your jumper at all and I'm certainly not a stretched zebra. That was all just tish-tosh. So come on, Brov. Chop-zip...I mean, zip-chop! Oh, I don't know what I mean any more. All I know is that if you keep crying you'll make me cry as well. Oh, bother! It's enough to make me scream –'

And then she had an idea!

'That's it, Brov!' she cried. 'Remember what Miss Whisper said about things getting on top of us? How we should dig a hole with the meteorite spoon and scream into it! Well, if ever things were on top of us then they're on top of us now.'

As if to prove the point, the shouting from upstairs grew suddenly much louder.

'Give me the spoon, Brov!' demanded Filly. 'I can feel some serious screaming coming on!'

Still sobbing, Fergal handed it to her.

Filly tried to dig a hole in the floor. But it was made of concrete and was far too hard.

'Wah-wah-wah!'

'Don't panic, Brov.'

Next she tried the wall.

True, it was made of brick. But it was so old and

crumbly that, with a little prising, the bricks started to fall away.

Filly dug into the earth behind.

'Look, Brov!'

Fergal continued crying.

Filly continued digging.

And, above, Mr and Mrs Thunder continued arguing.

Another brick fell away.

Then another.

The hole got bigger and bigger.

'It's time to scream, Brov!' announced Filly, when she was happy with the size of the hole. She stuck her head into it and, 'Ahhhhhhh!'

'Wah-wah-wah!' continued Fergal

'Not "wah", Brov,' Filly corrected him. 'It's "Ahhhhhhh". That's how you scream. And, I must say, I already feel a lot better for doing it. This meteorite spoon really does work. Now, you come and have a try before those tears of yours shrink your jumper to the size of a woolly hat.'

Slowly, Fergal approached the hole.

'Go on, Brov,' Filly urged.

Fergal took a deep breath, but all he could manage was a feeble, 'Wah-wah-wah!'

'A good first effort, Brov,' encouraged Filly. 'Try sticking your head right in the hole.'

'Wah-wah-wahhhhh!'

'You're getting there, Brov!'

'Wah-wah-waaahhhhhh!'

'One more time, Brov.'

And then it happened –

'AAAAAAAHHHHHHHHHHHHHHHH!' went Fergal.

Fergal's scream was the loudest scream Filly had ever heard. In fact, it was probably the loudest

scream ever screamed into a hole in The Whole History of Screaming into Holes.

And then something else happened –

The ceiling started to shake!

Cracks appeared in the walls!

The floor started to tremble!

And the whole cellar jumped up and down as if there was an earthquake.

Fergal dropped the meteorite spoon.

Dust filled the air.

Filly and Fergal were just about to shriek, when –

CRRRRRRRAAAAAAAASSSSSSSSHHHHHHH!

– there was the biggest crashing noise they'd ever heard.

It was probably – yes, you've guessed it! – the biggest crashing noise in The Whole History of Crashing Noises.

And then everything went very quiet.

And very, very dark...

10

In order to explain what had caused the biggest crashing noise in The Whole History of Crashing Noises, we'll have to go back upstairs.

You see, after Filly had followed Fergal down into the cellar, Mr and Mrs Thunder continued arguing.

They were still at the top of the stairs, insulting each other.

'You lipsticked lump of laziness!'

'You flaking fossil of dandruff!'

'You greying grubbiness of tangles!'

'You washed-out weed of waxiness!'

And then Mrs Thunder started to run down the stairs.

'And where do you think you're going?' demanded Mr Thunder.

'I don't need to pack a suitcase,' Mrs Thunder told him. 'I'M LEAVING YOU NOW!'

'*YOU'RE* NOT LEAVING *ME*!' cried Mr Thunder. '*I'M* LEAVING *YOU*!'

And, once more, they started to push past each other on the stairs.

Only this time...going down!

'OUT OF MY WAY!' yelled Mr Thunder.

'OUT OF MY WAY!' yelled Mrs Thunder.

They rushed to the bottom of the stairs.

Now they started to push past each other down the hallway, each one trying to get to the front door first.

Mr Thunder hollered, 'I WANT TO LEAVE YOU SO MUCH I COULD CHEW MY LIPS OFF!'

Mrs Thunder hollered, 'I WANT TO LEAVE YOU SO MUCH I COULD SUCK MY TEETH OUT!'

They both reached the front door at the same time.

They both opened the door.

They both rushed forward.

And, as a result, they both got stuck in the doorway!

'NINCOMPOOP!'

'NUMBSKULL!'

It was night now and very dark and quiet outside.

Mr and Mrs Thunder wriggled and squirmed and – with one almighty heave – managed to dislodge themselves.

They staggered into the darkness outside.

Mr Thunder grabbed hold of the door to slam it.

Mrs Thunder grabbed hold of the door to slam it.

And – together – they slammed it shut with as much force as humanly possible.

And that's when it happened!

A crack appeared above the front door. A very large crack. It shot up the side of the house and joined on to another crack –

This crack joined another crack.

Then another.

Another.

Suddenly, the cracks were like black snakes crawling all over the house.

The house started to wobble!

Mr and Mrs Thunder took a few steps back.

The cracks continued to join up...

A brick fell!

Then a window-ledge!

Then a slate from the roof!

'OUR HOME!' shrieked Mr and Mrs Thunder.

And then – with the biggest crashing noise in The Whole History of Crashing Noises – the Thunder house fell to the ground!

11

'Brov?'

'Yep, Sis?'

'Are you all right?'

'Yep, Sis.'

'Where are you, Brov?'

'Here, Sis.'

'It's too dark, Brov. I can't see a thing! I wonder what happened. Now, don't panic, Brov. I think I can feel my way to the cellar door...Yes, here are the steps up...Careful, careful...Here's the door. I'm turning the handle now, Brov. We'll be out any second. Crikey, Brov! The door won't open! And I can't see any light through the keyhole either. There must be something blocking the door from the other side. Now don't panic ... I'll just feel my way

down ...Careful, careful ...There. Crikey, Brov! Look! There's a light!'

A bright, golden light was coming from the hole that had been dug with the meteorite spoon.

Filly could see Fergal now.

There was dirt in his hair and his eyes were still red from sobbing but – apart from that – he looked fine.

Hand in hand, they approached the hole.

It was a lot larger now – as big as a doorway almost – and...well, it wasn't just a hole any more.

It was the entrance to a tunnel!

And a very long tunnel at that!

'Crikey!' gasped Filly.

'Yep, Sis!' agreed Fergal. And he grabbed Filly's hand and stepped forward –

'Wait, Brov!' warned Filly. 'Not so zip-zip, if you please. We've got to think about this. We can't just go strolling into any old tunnel that comes along.

We don't know what might be at the other end. It might be dangerous.'

'Nope, Sis,' insisted Fergal. And he took another step forward, pulling Filly with him.

I don't suppose we really have a choice, thought Filly. We can't get out through the cellar door. And I don't want to stay in the dark. Besides, that golden light does look very inviting.

'Righto, Brov,' she said, following. 'But let's be careful.'

The sides of the tunnel were dark earth and the ground was covered with brick-dust.

With each step the golden light got brighter and brighter. So bright, in fact, that it momentarily dazzled Filly and she had to rub her eyes. When her vision had finally cleared she noticed a strange thing.

The brick-dust was turning to –

'Sand, Brov!' exclaimed Filly, bending to scoop up a handful. 'Yellow sand!'

Fergal began to shuffle from side to side with excitement.

They walked on a little further.

And then Filly heard something.

'It can't be!' she said. 'But that noise! It sounds just like the – '

'Sea, Sis!' interrupted Fergal, shuffling more than ever. He'd seen programmes about the sea on television (before Mr Thunder had kicked the screen in, of course) and he could barely contain his excitement.

Filly's curiosity got the better of her and she started walking faster and faster.

The light got brighter.

The sound of the sea got louder.

There was more and more sand.

And then, all of a sudden, they rushed out of the tunnel and –

'Crikey!'

'Yep, Sis!'

They were standing on a beach. Yellow sand for as far as the eye could see. And there was the sea, crystal clear and as blue as the sky. A cloudless sky with a brilliant, golden sun. And there were palm trees. Tall palm trees with coconuts at the top.

And there was a sign. A sign with three words written on it. The words were:

Welcome to Honeymoonia

12

Mr and Mrs Thunder stared at the fallen house. For a while they were too shocked to move. There was nothing left but a pile of rubble.

A gentle breeze sent a few torn pieces of wallpaper fluttering into the night.

Apart from that everything was still.

And silent.

Until –

'MY SWEETHEARTS!' wailed Mrs Thunder.

'MY KIDDYWINKS!' wailed Mr Thunder.

And the two of them rushed forward and started digging through the debris.

'You did this, you nincompoop!' accused Mrs Thunder. 'It was you who slammed the door!'

'You slammed the door too, you numbskull!' insisted Mr Thunder.

'My poor sweethearts!' continued Mrs Thunder, throwing some bricks aside. 'They could be flat as pancakes for all we know.' She instinctively added a

quick, 'UGH!' at the thought of it, then went on, 'And it's all because you couldn't eat your nincompooping egg properly –'

'Just start digging!' interrupted Mr Thunder. 'I'm sure I saw them go down to the cellar. If that's so, we've got a long way to go. So just dig. There's no time for arguments now!'

'Nincompoop,' muttered Mrs Thunder under her breath, digging.

'Numbskull,' muttered Mr Thunder under his breath, digging.

And so it went on.

'Nincompoop.'

Digging.

'Numbskull.'

Digging.

'Nincompoop.'

Digging.

'Numbskull.'

Digging.

13

'Come on, Sis!' said Fergal, walking across the sand.

And, for a moment, Filly followed him, too surprised by what was around her to realize just how many words Fergal had said.

She looked behind her. The entrance to the tunnel was in a rock-face, like a cave.

Filly thought, Mustn't forget where this is. After all, we'll have to find our way back –

Then it hit her!

'Brov!' she exclaimed. 'You said three words!'

'I know that, Sis.'

'Four words!'

'Don't make a fuss, Sis.'

'Five!'

'Why keep on about it, Sis?'

'Six! And I keep on about it because I've never heard you say more than two words! Not ever! And now – why, now whole sentences are tumbling out! Why start now, Brov?'

'Because I've never been here before, Sis,' he explained, looking round at the sand and sea and palm trees.

'Seven words! Crikey, Brov! You'll be making speeches next – '

'Give that sea air a good sniff, Sis.' Fergal pulled the jumper off his nose and sniffed as deeply as he could.

'Eight!' gasped Filly. 'And your nose on show too! Crikey! As if it's not enough to find myself on a beach, I've got your nose and endless jabbering to contend with. I feel quite giddy with it all, Brov, I don't mind telling you.' She wiped sweat from her forehead with the cuff of her jumper. 'I hope I'm not going to get sunstroke as well!' she continued. 'Brov, let's sit down for a while. I need to collect my thoughts.'

They sat on the sand and stared out at the ocean.

Waves gently lapped against the shore. Multi-coloured seashells gleamed like jewels in the sunlight. It was so beautiful and peaceful.

Fergal continued breathing deeply for a while, then said, 'If I say something, please don't count my words.'

'Righto, Brov,' Filly assured him. She was feeling a little better now. Then, before she realized it, had counted, 'Nine!'

'Sis!' Fergal was upset. 'You said you wouldn't!'

'I could bite my tongue, Brov, really I could,' apologized Filly. 'I promise it won't happen again. Now, say what you were gong to say.'

Fergal took a deep breath. 'I was just wondering,' he began, gazing at the sea, 'if there were any dolphins –'

But he didn't get any further.

Because, suddenly, the sea was alive with dolphins.

They jumped out of the water and did somersaults in the air.

'There're hundreds of them, Sis!' giggled Fergal.

'Thousands, Brov!' said Filly, laughing.

'Millions, Sis!'

'Billions, Brov!'

'Trillions, Sis!'

'Zillions, Brov!'

'Squillions, Sis!'

The dolphins were flying out of the ocean like silver, wingless birds, some somersaulting, some skimming backwards across the surface of the water on the tips of their tails. The whole thing looked like a meticulously rehearsed display. Twenty dolphins would leap up simultaneously, all moving in the same direction, while twenty others would leap up elsewhere, all moving in the opposite direction, while others frolicked on their tails below.

Filly and Fergal clapped until their hands started to tingle and turn red.

Then, gradually, the dolphins disappeared beneath the waves.

'I don't know what to say, Brov,' admitted Filly. 'I've never seen anything like that before. I've no idea what's happening here. But, Brov, isn't it...gorgeous?'

'Wonderful, Sis,' Fergal agreed. He looked up at the sky. 'I'm wondering something else now.'

'What's that, Brov?'

'If there are any birds –'

But, again, he didn't get a chance to finish.

Because – and you guessed it! – a bird flew out of the sky and hovered above them. It was bright red with black eyes and a long, pointed beak.

'Crikey, Bro –' began Filly.

But she didn't finish either.

Because now there were two birds.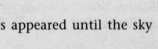

Then three.

Then four.

Five.

Six.

Seven.

More and more birds appeared until the sky

was so full of them they blocked out the sun.

'Gorgeous!'

'Wonderful!'

And, indeed, the birds were both of these things.

Some had red feathers, some yellow, some blue. Some had different colours on different parts of their body: pink wings with scarlet heads, purple breasts with emerald tails, lemon plumes with orange necks. Some had long feathers, some had tiny feathers, and some were multicoloured and highly decorated: turquoise spots with mauve stripes and snow-white diamonds, or snow-white stripes with mauve spots and turquoise diamonds, or even mauve diamonds with turquoise stripes and snow-white spots.

The birds hovered for a few moments, then – at exactly the same time – they all flew to the left. The collective sounds of their wings and squalling made Filly and Fergal's ears ring.

Then the birds flew to the right.

Then up.

Then down.

Around in a circle.

And all the time moving in unison, as if all their minds were connected by some invisible thread.

Some of their feathers fluttered to the sand below like a colourful snowstorm.

One feather went up Fergal's nose and he had to sneeze several times before it came out.

'That's what you get for letting your nose out of your jumper,' Filly teased him.

After a while the birds flew inland and settled in the jungle of palm trees.

'I'm speechless again, Brov,' Filly confessed once more. 'There seems to be no end of things that might make me say, "Crikey!" You wonder about dolphins – and there're dolphins! You wonder about birds – and there're birds! Perhaps I should try it. I wonder if...if there's a couple of plates of steak and chips so we can stop our stomachs rumbling!'

Filly waited...but nothing happened.

'I don't seem to have the knack, Brov,' Filly sighed. 'Why don't you have a go?'

'I will, Sis. But I'm not wondering about steak and chips. I'm wondering if there's anyone else –'

A man's voice interrupted him.

'You two hungry?' it called.

For a moment they couldn't see where it was coming from. Not on the beach. Not out at sea.

And then they saw him!

He was at the very top of a nearby palm tree,
picking coconuts.

Filly and Fergal started to walk towards him.

'He's wearing Bermuda shorts, Brov!' noticed Filly.

'And a Hawaiian shirt, Sis!' noticed Fergal.

As they got closer they noticed other things.

'Flip-flops, Brov!'

'Sunglasses, Sis!'

'And... he's got a suntan, Brov!'

'And a black quiff, Sis!'

'And lots of muscles, Brov!' Filly took a deep breath. 'Crikey!' she said in a faint voice. 'It can't be! But...he looks just like...a...a...' She was too astonished to finish.

So Fergal did it for her.

'A young Dad!' he said.

Mr Thunder called, 'I've found something!'

Mrs Thunder rushed over and knelt beside him in the rubble. 'What is it?' she asked.

They were both covered in dust and dirt now, their fingernails broken with digging.

'It's...it's the stop-watch!' Mr Thunder replied. 'The one Fergal always had on him. My poor little kiddywink.' Tears brimmed in his eyes. 'What was it I called him?'

'A squashed-in-his-jumper excuse of a boy!'

'Oh, don't remind me.'

'But you asked!'

'I know I did,' sighed Mr Thunder. 'But it breaks my heart to think of it. Oh, Fergal, Fergal...' He kissed the stop-watch. 'I'll never call you a squashed-in-your-jumper boy again. Or any other name. I promise, I promise.' Tears trickled down his cheeks.

Mrs Thunder wiped them away with the hem of her dressing-gown.

'Where's my comb?' Mr Thunder reached for his pocket.

'No time for that!' uttered Mrs Thunder, slapping his wrist. 'Who cares about your bald spot? We've got to keep digging. That's all! Keep digging!'

Mr Thunder nodded. 'Right you are,' he said. 'Keep digging!'

And that's what they did!

'We're very hungry!' Filly called to the man. 'Right, Brov?'

'Yep, Sis.'

'Then bombs away!' announced the man.

A coconut started falling.

'Look out, Sis!' warned Fergal.

They darted out of its path just in time. The coconut landed with a dull thud right where they'd been standing. They hardly had time to collect their thoughts before another coconut was dropped, and they had to dash out of the way once more.

'Careful up there!' warned Filly.

But all the man said was, 'Bombs away!' and yet another coconut fell.

Thud!

This one landed so close to Filly that its hairs tickled her nose as it whizzed past.

The man climbed down the tree and gave them a wide grin. 'It takes muscles to climb a tree like that,' he boasted. 'And I've got muscles by the truckload. Feel my arm.'

Filly and Fergal did as they were asked.

'What do you feel?' demanded the man.

'Muscles,' replied Filly.

'Right you are! Now feel my legs. What do you feel there?'

'Muscles on top of muscles,' replied Fergal.

'I'm like that all over. I've got muscles in places most people haven't even got places. And eating coconuts is good for building muscles. So – let's eat!'

He cracked the coconuts open on a nearby rock. He gave one to Filly, one to Fergal, and the third he

ate himself.

Fergal pulled the jumper all the way off his face now.

Filly would have said, 'Crikey! His chin!' but she was too busy eating and, besides, so many astounding things had happened she wasn't sure if she could be astounded enough to say, 'Crikey!' any more.

'You know what coconuts are?' demanded the man.

'Good for muscles?' suggested Fergal.

'Apart from that.'

Filly and Fergal shook their heads.

'They're wunnerful!' he told him. 'That's what they are. One of many wunnerful things on the island. And you want to know what the most wunnerful thing out of all the wunnerful things is?'

'The sunshine?' tried Filly.

'No.'

'The sand?' tried Fergal.

'No.'

'The dolphins?'

'No.'

'The birds?'

'No, no, no, no, no.' The man had finished his coconut now and threw the shell to one side. 'What I'm talking about is *so* wunnerful that, in comparison, the sun is a light-bulb and the sand is brick-dust and the dolphins are pickled herrings and the birds are bluebottle flies.'

'Then what is it?' asked Filly.

'Mrs Love!'

'What – I mean, *who* is Mrs Love?'

'Well, let me give you a clue,' said the man, smirking. 'I am ...Mr Love!'

'So Mrs Love is your wife!'

'Right you are!'

'Where is she?' Fergal wanted to know.

'She's sunbathing. Just along the beach. She's getting more suntanned and wunnerful by the second. Oh, Mrs Love...Mrs Love...' His eyes got all dreamy. 'Everything about her makes my body go ping and zap. And here – feel my heart.' He pressed Filly's hand against his chest. 'How's it going?'

'Boom-boom,' Filly replied.

'Right you are! You know what Mrs Love was put

on this planet to do?'

'Love you?' suggested Filly.

'Right you are! And you know what I'm going to give her?'

'The rest of your life?'

'Right you are! And you know what I'll always be when I'm with her?'

'A spring chicken?'

Mr Love smiled and nodded. 'Oh, love is a wunnerful thing! It feels like fizzy drink has been poured all over your body and bouncy springs attached to the soles of your feet.' And he trembled all over, obviously enjoying the fizzy bounciness of

it all. Then, abruptly, he slapped his thighs (his muscles on muscles thighs) and announced, 'I'm going to make a huge heart in the sand, out of seashells. And then I'll write MR LOVE LOVES MRS LOVE in the middle. But I'll have to be quick! She'll be finishing her sunbathing soon.'

'We'll help you,' Fergal told him. 'Yep, Sis?'

'Right, Brov!'

'Right you are! Hang on! I've been so busy telling you to feel my muscles and about the light of my life, I haven't even asked what your names are yet.'

'I'm Fergal,' Fergal informed him. 'And this is my sister, Filly.'

But Mr Love's mind was obviously still full of muscles and love. Because all he did was grin inanely and say, 'Let's make a heart, Frenny and Farley.'

16

Mrs Thunder called, 'Look what I've found!'

Mr Thunder rushed over and knelt beside her in the rubble. 'What is it?' he asked.

'It's...it's a tube of glue!' Mrs Thunder replied. 'The glue Filly was always sticking things together with. Oh, my poor little sweetheart.' Tears brimmed in Mrs Thunder's eyes. 'What was it I called her?'

'A stretched zebra!'

'Oh, don't remind me.'

'But you asked!'

'I know I did,' sighed Mrs Thunder. 'But it breaks my heart to think of it. Oh, Filly, Filly...' She kissed the glue. 'I'll never call you a stretched zebra again. Or any other name. I promise, I promise.' Tears trickled down her cheeks.

Mr Thunder wiped them away with the hem of his dressing-gown.

'Where's my lipstick?' began Mrs Thunder, reaching for her pocket.

'No time for that!' uttered Mr Thunder, slapping her wrist. 'Who cares if you haven't got any lips. We've got to keep digging. That's all! Keep digging!'

Mrs Thunder nodded. 'That's right,' she said. 'Keep digging!'

And that's what they did!

17

The seashells were many different shapes and sizes: some were cone-shaped and bright pink, some were round and yellow, some star-shaped and blue as the sky.

'They're so wonderful, Sis!' remarked Fergal, picking one up. 'Look at this!'

It was lime green with yellow flecks and was, by far, the biggest they'd found.

'You know what they say, Brov?' said Filly. 'If you put a shell to your ear you can hear the sea.'

'But I can hear the sea already!' insisted Fergal, pointing at the ocean.

'You can hear another sea, then! Go on, try it, Brov!'

Fergal listened intently for a while, then started to frown. Slowly, he took the shell from his ear, shook his head as if unable to believe what he'd just heard, then had another listen. The frown grew deeper.

'Well, I can hear something all right, Sis,' he said at last. 'But it's not the sea!'

Filly grabbed the shell and put it to her own ear.

'Crikey, Brov!' She dropped the shell. 'You're right! That's not the sea at all! That's the sound of a crane swinging a ball and chain through the air and...and –'

'It's the sound of buildings being knocked down,' Fergal said.

They stared at each other in shock.

'Hurry up, you two!' called Mr Love. He was sitting on a nearby rock. 'No time to dawdle. We've got a heart to make!'

'Righto!' Filly called back, still a little shaken.

And they resumed collecting seashells, trying
as hard as possible to forget the sound the shells
contained.

It was tiring work beneath the hot sun, made even more tiring by the fact that Mr Love didn't help at all. He just sat on the rock, sighing, 'Mrs Love...Mrs Love...' over and over again. Occasionally he would glance across and compliment Filly and Fergal on their endeavours, but as for actually putting in some elbow-grease...oh no! Not him!

'There's a shell just by your foot, Mr Love,' Filly told him. 'Can you bring it over? That one should just about finish the heart.'

'Mrs Love...Mrs Love...' he continued sighing, apparently not hearing.

With an impatient sigh, Filly got the shell herself and slammed it in place. 'There!' she exclaimed. 'Heart complete!'

On hearing this, Mr Love jumped to his feet. 'Wunnerful!' he cried. And, with his finger, wrote MR LOVE LOVES MRS LOVE in the middle of the heart, then stood back to admire it. 'Mrs Love will be so pleased,' he commented. 'I'm so glad I made her –'

'*You* made!' gasped Filly. 'All you did was sit on that rock and –'

'MR LOVE!' a new voice called.

A woman's voice!

'MRS LOVE!' Mr Love called back, his whole face lighting up as if a light-bulb had just been switched on somewhere inside.

And there she was! There was Mrs Love, rushing across the sand towards Mr Love as if her life depended on it.

'She's wearing Bermuda shorts, Sis!' noticed Fergal.

'And a Hawaiian shirt, Brov!' noticed Filly.

Mrs Love got closer and closer...

'Flip-flops, Sis!'

'Sunglasses, Brov!'

'Suntan, Sis!'

'And long wavy hair, Brov!'

'And a narrow waist, Sis.' Fergal took a deep breath. 'I might as well say it,' he said. 'She looks just like a young Mum!'

Suddenly Mrs Love tripped. One of her flip-flops

came off and she staggered right into the waiting arms of Mr Love.

'My cosmic piece of suntanned crackling!' cried Mr Love. 'Did you hurt yourself?'

'I walked across the hot sand, my galactically glorious tower of muscle!' she replied, clutching her foot. 'And look! There! I've got a blister on my little toe – UGH!'

'It's not "ugh" in the least, my shimmering morning blossom.' And Mr Love bent down, took her foot in his hands and started blowing on her burnt toe. 'This will take away any stinging, my darling with the dainty feet.'

'Ooooooo,' quivered Mrs Love, as his breath touched her skin. 'Ooooooo – how I missed you while I was sunbathing, my wild-breathed stallion.'

'It's only been thirty minutes, my blister-toed gazelle!'

'But thirty minutes is thirty hours when I'm not with you, my sizzling fillet of spicy beefcake.'

'And thirty hours is thirty days without you, my universal uniqueness!'

'And thirty days is thirty years without you, my swaggering swashbuckler!'

'Thirty years is thirty decades!'

'Thirty decades is thirty thousand years!'

'Thirty thousand years is thirty million years!'

'Thirty million years is thirty billion years!'

'Thirty billion years is thirty trillion years!'

'Thirty trillion years is thirty zillion years!'

'Thirty zillion years is thirty squillion years!'

Crikey! thought Filly. They do make a song and dance of it all.

'How's your toe now, my luscious-lipped fancy?' asked Mr Love, gently kissing it.

'Much better,' came the reply. 'And all thanks to you, my quiff-tipped quiver-maker. I don't know how you can bring yourself to kiss that blister.'

'Because anything that's part of you is immediately wunnerful, that's how,' Mr Love told her. 'Your toes are wunnerful!' He kissed each one in turn. 'Your ankles are wunnerful!' More kisses. 'Your shins are wunnerful!' Kisses, kisses. 'Your knees are –'

'Oh, just show her the heart!' snapped Filly impatiently. She'd seen more than enough of all this silly kissing, thank you very much.

Mrs Love noticed Filly and Fergal for the first time. 'Where did you two spring from?' she asked.

'We've been here all along actually,' Filly informed her flatly. 'Only you were too busy... doing other things.'

'My perennial love,' began Mr Love, 'let me introduce you. This is...er...Fweenie and ... er...'

'I'm Filly,' interrupted Filly curtly. 'And this is Fergal, my brother. And over here is the seashell heart that –'

'Heart!' cried Mrs Love, rushing over to it. 'It's the most gorrrjusss thing I've ever seen! Oh, my love, my love, my love.' She rushed back to Mr Love and – you've guessed it! – they started kissing again.

The kisses were getting more slurpy by the second.

Here we go again! thought Filly.

'Did you do all that just for me, you suntanned matinée idol?' Slurp-kiss-slurp. 'What a lot of work!' Kiss-slurp-kiss. 'You must have worn those huge manly hands right to the bone!'

Filly was just about to say that it wasn't his huge manly hands, but their tiny children's hands, but she didn't get a chance because –

'A boat trip!' Mrs Love suddenly blurted out.

'Wh-what was that, my love?' asked Mr Love, still in the middle of the slurpiest kiss so far.

'I feel like a boat trip,' explained Mrs Love. 'Please go and get the row-boat for me, my killer-shark dream-machine.'

'Anything for you, my tasty morsel,' he assured her, wiping post-kiss slurp from his chin and neck. 'But why don't you come with me to get it. I'll be lonely without you.'

'No, I'll stay here and talk to...what are your names again?'

'Filly and Fergal,' said Filly firmly.

Mrs Love ran her fingers through Mr Love's hair. 'But don't be long, my chunk of a hunk.'

Mr Love ran to get the row-boat. Every few steps, however, he turned, blew a kiss and called, 'I miss you already!' And every time he did this Mrs Love blew a kiss and called, 'I miss you too!' after him.

This went on for as long as Mr Love was in sight.

Then Mrs Love sighed and clutched her chest.

'Oh, Mr Love ... Mr Love...' Her eyes got all dreamy. 'Everything about him makes my body go fizz and pop. And you know how he makes my heart go?'

'Pitty-pat?' Fergal and Filly replied together.

'That's right! And you know what Mr Love was put on this planet to do?'

'Love you?' they replied.

'That's right! And you know what I'm going to give him?'

'The rest of your life?'

'That's right! And you know what I'll always be when I'm with him?'

'A spring chicken?'

'That's right! And now, you know what I'm going to do?'

Filly and Fergal had to shake their heads at this one.

'I'm going to make a huge heart out of seashells to surprise him. And I'm going to write MRS LOVE LOVES MR LOVE in the middle. That's why I sent Mr Love to get a row-boat. But I'll have to be quick. You'll help me, won't you?'

'Do you promise to actually *help* make the heart?' Filly asked. 'You won't just let us do all the work while you sit on a rock and sigh "Mr Love" over and over again?'

'Of course I won't,' said Mrs Love, smiling.

Mr Thunder said, 'There's a large slab of concrete here! It's too heavy for me!'

'Let me help you,' said Mrs Thunder.

And that's what she did.

And, with her help, the concrete was shifted.

'I've never worked so hard,' panted Mr Thunder. 'Look! Sweat is trickling down my face!'

'Me too,' panted Mrs Thunder. 'I'm sweating so much my clothes are stuck to me. But we've got no choice! We've got to keep digging – Wait! Now *I've* found a large slab of concrete. It's too heavy for *me*!'

'Let me help you,' said Mr Thunder.

And that's what he did.

And, with his help, the concrete was shifted.

And that's how they continued digging – helping each other.

But – of course – Mrs Love didn't help Filly and Fergal build the heart at all!

'What a fibber she is!' hissed Fergal, glaring at Mrs Love on the rock.

Filly and Fergal rushed all over the place collecting shells. It was a little more difficult now, as most of the shells had been used to make the first heart. They had to run further and further to find new ones. Before long, they were both so breathless they could hardly speak.

'I'm...sweating...so much,' panted Fergal, '...my jumper...is stuck...to me!'

Filly panted, 'So much...of my sweat...has trickled into my boots...it feels like...I'm paddling!'

'We should...go with them...on their row-boat,' said Fergal, putting a shell in place. 'That would...cool us down.'

'Hurry up, you two!' Mrs Love told them. 'No time for gossiping! We've got a heart to make!'

Fergal looked at Filly. 'I don't know...about you, Sis,' he said, 'but I think...all this love stuff ... is exhausting!'

'Ditto, Brov – Crikey! I think we're running...out of shells'

'There're some over there...by those palm trees, Sis.'

And they went to get them.

They were just putting the final shell in place when they heard, 'MRS LOVE! MRS LOVE!'

A tiny row-boat was making its way inshore towards them. Mr Love was rowing as fast as he could.

Mrs Love jumped to her feet and waved. Then she shot Filly and Fergal a look. 'Heart ready?' she asked.

'It is,' replied Filly. 'No thanks to you!'

As quickly as she could, Mrs Love scrawled MRS LOVE LOVES MR LOVE in the centre, then rushed into the sea to greet Mr Love. Mr Love jumped out of the boat to meet her halfway and, knee-deep in waves, they started all that slurpy kissing once again.

'They're going to wear their lips out if they're not careful,' remarked Filly. 'I've never seen so much soppiness in all my born days. Crikey – Mr Love's seen the heart now!'

Mr Love was splashing through the water towards them. 'A heart!' he cried. 'It's the most wunnerful thing I've ever seen. Oh, my love, my love, my love!' He rushed back to Mrs Love and...well, need I say?

Slurp-kiss-slurp.

'How fast you made it, my mermaid of the sands,'

he salivated. 'Your dainty fingers making things for me!' Kiss-slurp-kiss. 'You could have given yourself a blister on your finger as well as on your toe –'

'*WE* MADE THE HEART!' yelled Filly. All that kissing and slurping had finally got to her and she'd blown her top. 'THAT'S WHY OUR JUMPERS ARE STUCK TO US AND OUR BOOTS ARE FULL OF SWEAT! NOW, I'M GETTING FED UP WITH ALL YOUR SOPPINESS. YOU DON'T NOTICE ANYTHING BUT EACH OTHER. ALL THAT KISSING AND SLURPING IS DISGUSTING! ALL MUMS AND DADS KISS AND SLURP, I KNOW, BUT I'VE NEVER SEEN ANYONE DO IT AS MUCH AS YOU! I BET YOU KISS AND SLURP MORE THAN ANYONE IN THE WHOLE HISTORY OF KISSING AND SLURPING! NOW, I WANT YOU TO STOP ACTING LIKE A COUPLE OF NOODLES AND LISTEN TO WHAT *WE* WANT FOR A CHANGE!' She took a deep breath and calmed down a little. 'We want a boat trip. We need to cool off and get unstuck. Once we've had a boat trip you can do a bit more kissing and slurping if you like. But, until then, you give *us* some time. Right, Brov?'

Fergal had never heard Filly speak like this. For a moment he just stared at her. Then he managed, 'Yep, Sis!'

Mr and Mrs Love were also staring. They looked totally dumbfounded. Finally, though, in a tremulous voice, Mrs Love asked, 'Have...have we been kissing too much?'

'Much too much!' Filly maintained. 'You can't even remember our names because you're too busy slurping. Well, can you? Chop-chop! What are they?'

Mrs Love thought for a while.

'Er...Foggy and Fargy?' she guessed.

'No.'

Now Mr Love had a go. 'Figgy and Frally?'

'No, no, no!' muttered Filly crossly. 'Our names are Filly and Fergal. Say them!'

'Filly and Fergal,' murmured Mr and Mrs Love.

'And please don't forget! Now...you're going to take us out on the boat. Right?'

'That's right...Filly,' said Mrs Love. Then added, 'And ... I didn't realize we were being so selfish. Did you, Mr Love?'

'No, Mrs Love.'

'And it won't happen again. Will it, Mr Love?'

'No, Mrs Love. Now let's get you cooled off ... Filly and Fergal.'

Mr Love picked Filly and Fergal up and took them to the boat. Once they were all inside, Mr Love took one oar and Mrs Love took the other and, together, they rowed out to sea.

Filly and Fergal looked over the edge of the boat. The water was so clear they could see all the way to the bottom.

'Wonderful!' breathed Fergal, letting his hand trail in the water.

'Gorgeous!' breathed Filly, also trailing a hand.

A dolphin did a somersault beside them.

Mr and Mrs Love were smiling at each other.

Everything was just right between them.

There was no fear of shouting or anything breaking.

It felt like a time that Filly had only known for a brief while, and Fergal had never known at all.

It felt like being loved and looked after properly.

It was the safest and best feeling in The Whole History of Safe and Best Feelings.

Fergal looked at Filly and smiled.

She could tell he was feeling the same as her. He had never looked so peaceful.

'This is what it should always be like, Brov,' Filly said.

'I want it to go on for ever, Sis.'

'Ditto, Brov.'
And perhaps it would have.
Only, suddenly, Fergal pointed at something...
It was at the bottom of the sea.
Filly peered at it.
A hazy, dark shape.
'A wreck!' she gasped. 'A shipwreck!'
But then she saw it more clearly...
Saw a brick wall!
A kitchen window!
A television aerial!
'It's not a *ship*wreck at all,' said Filly. 'It's a –'
'*House*wreck!' said Fergal.

20

Mr and Mrs Thunder both found something at exactly the same time. Mr Thunder grabbed one end of it, while Mrs Thunder grabbed the other.

'What is it?' asked Mrs Thunder.

'I'm not sure,' came the reply.

They pulled it from the debris.

'It's...it's a book!' said Mr Thunder. He brushed dust from the cover. '*The Book of Arguments*,' he read.

'I think that's Filly's handwriting,' commented Mrs Thunder.

They looked at each other and frowned.

Then started turning the pages...

'It's...it's about *us*!' gasped Mrs Thunder. 'Look! There!' She read, '*Mum and Dad broke a lot of things in this argument, but I will call it "The Argument that Broke the Telephone", as that was the first thing to get smashed. From now on the first thing to get broken will give the argument its title.*'

'Title!' cried Mr Thunder, horrified. 'They gave our arguments titles?' He turned to another page and read, '*Dad called Mum a stinking old cauliflower-dollop. This is a new insult from what I know. Mum didn't come up with any new insults, but she put on so much lipstick afterwards her face was like a red traffic-light.*'

Mrs Thunder turned a page: '*Date: Monday 13 December ... Length of time before first argument: three minutes.* Oh, it can't be! Surely not! We must have been awake longer than three minutes before we started arguing.' She was too shocked to carry on reading.

Mr Thunder continued for her. '*Length of first argument: four hours and thirty minutes and ten seconds…Thing (or things) broken: the spin-drier…Title of argument: The Argument that Broke the Spin-drier. Cause of argument: Dad's smelly feet –'*

'Oh no!' interrupted Mrs Thunder in disbelief. 'We wouldn't quarrel about that! Surely not!'

'But we must have. It's all down here in black and white.'

Mrs Thunder clutched Mr Thunder's arm. 'This means that…they heard everything!' she cried. 'Every single shout!'

'Every single insult!' Mr Thunder clutched Mrs Thunder's arm.

'Every breaking thing!'

'Every slamming door!'

Mrs Thunder looked totally aghast. 'I...I feel so ashamed,' she said in a broken voice. 'What terrible parents we've been.'

'And they were such meaningless arguments,' commented Mr Thunder, his voice also breaking. 'What does it matter if my feet smell. I'll wash them. There's no need to shout the house down.'

Mrs Thunder sighed. 'We were so...stupid. We had a house. And children. Two wonderful children. And now...' She looked at the wreckage all round her. 'We've both been nincompoops!' she declared, clutching Mr Thunder tighter than ever.

'We've both been numbskulls!' agreed Mr Thunder, clutching Mrs Thunder just as tightly.

And their clutching grew tighter and closer and closer and tighter until it became an embrace.

'No more arguments!' said Mrs Thunder.

'No more arguments!' said Mr Thunder.

And they held each other for a few moments.

Then – at exactly the same time – they both exclaimed, 'Dig, my love!'

And they dug like they had never dug before.

21

'Ouch!' yelped Fergal.

'What's wrong, Brov?'

'A fish bit my finger!'

They'd been leaning over the edge of the boat, still trailing their hands in the water, and looking at the housewreck below. They'd managed to locate a bedroom window and the front door. And Filly was just about to point at the back door when Fergal let out his cry.

'Let me see, Fergal,' said Mrs Love, taking his hand in hers. She studied it carefully. 'It hasn't been bitten,' she told him. 'It's been stung! You see?' She pointed at a tiny needle sticking out of his fingertip. 'You've been needled by one of the Argument Fish, I'm afraid.'

'Argument Fish!' exclaimed Fergal.

'There's a lot of them in the sea. Bright red things covered in needles. Just like the one in your finger. Now I'll just pull it out for you.'

Fergal looked a little wary and tugged his hand away. 'Will it hurt?' he asked nervously.

'Not at all,' Mrs Love assured him. 'That's right, isn't it,

Mr Love?'

'Right you are, Mrs Love!'

Mrs Love took Fergal's hand again and looked at it more closely.

Mr Love put his arm round Fergal's shoulders and gave him a gentle squeeze. 'Look over there!' he said, pointing out to sea. 'Can you see all those dolphins?'

Fergal peered into the dazzling distance. 'I see them,' he replied. The sight of them made him smile.

'How many are there?'

'One...two...three...four...Ouch!'

'There!' grinned Mrs Love, holding the needle in the air. 'It's out! And you didn't feel a thing, did you?'

But Fergal didn't answer. He just glared at Mr and Mrs Love. Something was wrong with him. His face was turning red. His eyes were glaring. And he was snarling.

'Is it stinging?' asked Mr Love. 'Shall I blow on it for you – '

'No!' snapped Fergal angrily. 'I don't want your poo-breath all over me!'

'Brov!' Filly was shocked. 'What's wrong?'

Fergal continued glaring and snarling and getting even redder.

Mrs Love sighed. 'It's the needle, I'm afraid, Filly,' she said. 'They're poisoned with something that makes you...well, argue!'

'But... what can we do?'

'I really don't know. You see, neither Mr Love nor I has ever been stung.'

'But...what's the cure?'

'I don't think there is one.'

'No cure!' gasped Filly. 'So ... how long does it last?'

'I don't know that either,' replied Mrs Love. 'It could last a few minutes...or a few hours...or for ever!'

'For ever?' cried Filly.

Mr Love grabbed the oars and started rowing. 'We'll have to get back to shore,' he told them. 'Fergal's rocking the boat too much.'

And, indeed, that's exactly what Fergal was doing. Stomping his feet and muttering under his breath.

'Do stop all this tish-tosh, Brov,' pleaded Filly.

'Don't you dare say "tish-tosh" to me!' snarled Fergal. 'You stretched zebra!'

Filly gasped.

'And don't tell me to "chop-chop"!' Fergal continued, 'or "zip-zip" or "don't dilly-dally" or any others of your ridiculous little sayings!'

'Brov!' gasped Filly. 'Please don't say nasty things –'

'Shut your mouth!' shouted Fergal, stamping his foot so hard Filly thought he might go right through the bottom of the boat. 'Don't ever speak to me again! I'm fed up with your chirpiness all the time! Always in a good mood! Always looking on the bright side of things –'

'But, Brov –'

'Shut your mouth...you ninny! That's what you are! A ninny. And you know what else I'm fed up with? All your "Time for the stop-watch, Brov" and "Time for the book, Brov" and "Time for the glue, Brov". Always bossing me about!'

'Bossing you about?' Filly had tears in her eyes now. 'But, Brov, I only did it for you –'

'Listen to yourself! You just can't stop talking! You rattle on and on like a broken record!'

Filly couldn't believe Fergal was speaking to her like this.

Is this what he really thinks of me? she thought. After all I've done to make his life easier? He just thinks I'm a...a broken record?

Mrs Love put her arm round Filly. 'Don't listen to him, Filly,' she said. 'It's the needle talking. Not him –'

'But it *is* him!' sobbed Filly. 'It's my little Brov and... he thinks I'm...' She couldn't talk for crying.

'The waterworks are off now!' sneered Fergal. 'Wah-wah-wah! That's all you're good for, you ninny!'

'We're here!' said Mr Love, as the boat reached the shore.

'I'm leaving you!' yelled Fergal at Filly. 'I don't want to be your Brov any more and I don't want a bossy broken-record-of-a-thing like you for a Sis. If I never see you again it will be too soon! Goodbye!'

And, with that, he jumped out of the boat, marched across the sand and – muttering, 'Ninny!' over and over again – disappeared amongst the palm trees.

Filly watched him go, still weeping.

Mr and Mrs Love hugged her.

'You mustn't get upset,' said Mr Love.

'It will probably wear off soon,' said Mrs Love. 'And then Fergal will probably come back and he'll probably say he's sorry and everything will probably be back to normal.'

'So many probablys!' Filly exclaimed between sobs. 'Probably this!' Sob. 'Probably that!' Sob. 'But probably's not good enough!' Sob. 'I want my Brov back *definitely*.' Sob. 'Not probably!'

Mrs Love wiped Filly's face with a corner of her Hawaiian shirt. 'I wish there was something we could do,' she said sadly. 'Really I do.'

Mr Love nodded in agreement.

Gradually, Filly calmed down.

And a determined look came over her face.

'Righto,' she murmured. 'I know what to do.'

'What?' asked Mrs Love.

'I'm going after him.'

'Do you want us to come with you?'

'No,' replied Filly. 'Why don't you two do some more sunbathing? The sun's beginning to go down now so you haven't got much time left. Besides, what I have to do, I have to do *alone*!'

22

'There it is!' cried Mr Thunder.

'What?'

'The door to the cellar! Behind that large timber. See it?'

'Yes!' Mrs Thunder rushed over. 'My sweethearts!' she yelled. 'My sweethearts! Can you hear me?'

'My kiddywinks! My kiddywinks!' yelled Mr Thunder. 'Can you hear me?'

There was a long pause while they waited for a reply.

But none came.

'Do...do you think they're all right?' asked Mrs Thunder, her voice quivering.

'Of course they are!' Mr Thunder assured her. 'Now, help me! We've got to push the timber out of the way!'

They both started to push.

But it was very heavy and wouldn't budge.

'What are we going to do?' whimpered Mrs Thunder.

'Keep trying!' Mr Thunder told her firmly. 'We'll push together on the count of three. Push with every little bit of strength we've got. Ready?'

'Ready!'

'One...two...three...*Push*!'

The timber didn't move.

'Again!' said Mr Thunder. 'One ... two ... three ... *Push*!'

Nothing

'One...two...three...*Push*!'

Nothing.

'One ... two ... three ... *Push*!'

And it moved!
Only slightly...but still a move!
'We're doing it!' cried Mrs Thunder
'*Together* we are!' said Mr Thunder. 'Now, don't stop! One ... two ... three ...Push! Again! One ... two ... three ... *Push*!'
And they went on pushing.
Together!

23

Filly looked at the jungle all round her.

She'd left Mr and Mrs Love sunbathing on the beach and, for a while, had walked through the palm trees and foliage, calling, 'Brov!' without giving it a second thought.

Now, however, the second thoughts came.

And third and fourth thoughts, for that matter.

The sun was setting and the shadows were getting deeper and longer. The palm trees that had looked so exotic and inviting in broad daylight appeared more menacing now.

'Brov!' called Filly again. (Though not so boldly as before.)

Some birds erupted from the nearby trees at the sound of her voice.

Filly jumped.

Now just buck up, thought Filly. It's just some harmless birds, that's all. And...and so what if the sun is going down. Just look at the sky. What beautiful colours! Red, yellow, orange, scarlet and mauve! Just like a painting. There's no reason to be nervous. None at all.

'Brov!'

More fluttering birds.

Filly thought, I must remember my way back. It's getting darker by the second and I don't want to get lost in the jungle, thank you very much. Now, which way did I come?

She looked behind her.

It was basically through those two trees, she thought. And I can't miss *them*. They're probably the tallest palm trees in The Whole History of Tall Palm Trees...And then there's just a tiny stream to jump over and then it's just a little way to the beach. I only hope Brov isn't too far away now.

'Brov! Brov!'

Filly walked on a little further.

The leaves of the palm trees rustled in the gentle breeze.

She was just beginning to feel a little more confident, when she walked into a clearing and saw something.

Something that made her stop dead in her tracks.

Something that made her mouth gape open and

her eyes grow very wide.

'Volcano!' gasped Filly.

For that's what it was.

Rising high above the palm trees. A vast, threatening silhouette against the sunset. Smoke was rising from its gaping top.

That's all I need, thought Filly. Not only have I lost my Brov, not only is it getting darker by the second, but I've got a volcano to contend with as well. This is feeling less safe by the second.

She walked a little further.

'Brov!' she called nervously.

Fluttering birds.

'Brov!'

Birds.

'Brov!'

And then she heard his voice. 'Ninny!' he was muttering. 'Ninny! Ninny!'

She hurried in its direction and...

There he was!

Marching round and round a palm tree. 'Ninny!' he said again. 'Ninny!' He was still very red in the face, with bulging eyes and snarling lips. 'All her zip-zips!' he continued. 'In that silly chirpy voice – UGH! And her chop-chops – UGH! UGH! And as for her don't dilly-dallys and tish-toshes and crikeys – UGH! UGH! UGH!'

He's working himself into a right old state, thought Filly. I only hope my plan works. It should do. After all, when we're back home, saying 'Honeymoon' calms Mum and Dad down. So, now we're in Honeymoonia, saying 'Home' should have the same effect. Oh well, here goes –

'Home!' said Filly, stepping forward.

Fergal stopped marching round the tree and

looked at his sister.

Crikey! thought Filly. I think it's working!

'Home!' she said again, taking another step forward.

'Wh-what about it?' asked Fergal.

'Tell me about it,' Filly told him. 'What's it like?'

'It's ... a house,' he replied, wiping the spit from his lips.

'What kind of house?'

'It's...got a kitchen...and a hallway...and bedrooms.'

'How many bedrooms exactly?'

'Two.'

The redness started to fade from Fergal's face, his eyes lost their glare and the snarl uncurled from his lips.

Filly took a stop closer. 'Do you sleep in one of these bedrooms?' she asked.

'Yep,' Fergal replied. 'I sleep on a bottom bunk. It's very cosy. I have a blanket. The blanket's got a few holes in it. Sometimes my foot goes through one. But I don't mind.'

'If you sleep on the bottom bunk, who sleeps on the top one?'

'My Sis. She looks after me. She tries her best to cheer me up. If I have a nightmare she says, "Buck up, Brov! What tish-tosh those nightmares of yours are!"' Suddenly a look of recognition appeared on Fergal's face. He stared at Filly. 'Oh...what happened to me, Sis?' he asked. 'I said such nasty things to you! I'm so sorry, Sis! Really!' He gave her a big hug.

'Don't worry, Brov,' she assured him. 'It's all over and done with now.'

'But I didn't mean a word of it.'

'I know that, Brov. It was the needle that made you talk that way. Now don't upset yourself. Buck up – oh, I suppose I can still say buck up?' Filly smiled.

'Yep, Sis.'

'And zip-zip, Brov?'

'Yep, Sis.'

'And chop-chop and tish-tosh, Brov?'

'Say them all you like, Sis.'

'Buck up, buck up, buck up!' cried Filly, giggling. 'Zip-zip, zip-zip, zip-zip! Chop-chop, chop-chop, chop-chop! Tish-tosh, tish-tosh, tish-tosh!' She was laughing out loud now. 'You looked so funny when you were arguing, Brov!' she told him.

'Did I, Sis?'

'Oh yes. Your eyes went so wide I thought they'd pop right out of your head. And you went all red and your lips were...oh, so funny.'

Fergal laughed. 'Show me, Sis!'

Filly made her eyes go as wide as possible. 'Like

this!' she said. 'And your lips went...' And she pulled her lips back over her teeth. 'And your face went...' And she strained until her face was bright red.

Fergal was laughing so much he fell to the ground.

'And...' continued Filly, also falling, and laughing every bit as much as him, '...you called me a...a broken-record-of-a-thing!'

They laughed until they were too exhausted to laugh any more.

It was night now and the sky was full of stars.

Filly and Fergal lay on their backs and gazed up.

'So may stars, Sis,' said Fergal, softly 'There must be hundreds!'

'Thousands, Brov!'

'Millions, Sis!'

'Billions, Brov!'

'Trillions, Sis!'

'Zillions, Brov!'

'Oh, too many to count, Sis,' Fergal said. 'And there – look, Sis!'

A shooting star cut across the sky. And...yes, it was like the biggest firework in The Whole History of Fireworks.

'Wonderful!'

'Gorgeous!'

And then they saw something else.

At first they thought it might be the Moon, but the Moon is bright white and this...this was blue. And it was full of swirling shapes. Like a blue thumbprint against the heavens.

'It's the World, Sis!' exclaimed Fergal.

'The most gorgeous thing in The Whole History of Gorgeous Things,' said Filly.

'And the most wonderful too,' Fergal said. He took a deep breath. 'Sis...talking about home has made me realize...' His voice trailed away.

'Yes, Brov?' encouraged Filly.

'I miss Mum and Dad, Sis,' Fergal told her. 'Mr and Mrs Love are fine...but, well, they're not...'

'They're just not Mum and Dad.'

Fergal nodded. 'Yep, Sis,' he said. 'I miss our home. I miss everything. Well, I don't miss the arguments. But, perhaps, if we tell Mum and Dad just how much we don't like them – just like you told Mr and Mrs Love to stop all that slurpy kissing all the time – then…well, perhaps Mum and Dad will behave properly too.'

Filly nodded.

'So…' Fergal got to his feet. 'Time to go back, Sis?'

Filly stood up and smiled. 'Time to go back, Brov!'

Then they both said together, 'I want to go home!'

And that's when the volcano exploded!!!

Mr and Mrs Thunder continued to push the timber away from the cellar door.

Suddenly, Mrs Thunder lost her footing and slipped over.

As she fell, she grabbed hold of Mr Thunder and pulled him to the ground with her.

They landed with a heavy thud!

'Are you all right, my love?' asked Mr Thunder.

'Yes,' replied Mrs Thunder. 'Are you, my love?'

'Yes.'

'Then don't let's worry about us. We've got our sweethearts to find. One...two...three...Push!'

—25—

'Run, Brov!' cried Filly.

The volcano was spurting lava in all directions. Some of it shot straight up – turning the sky red – but most of it...

Most of it flowed down the side of the volcano like a wall of fire.

'I forget the way back, Sis!' Fergal was running as fast as he could to keep up with his sister. 'I...I was in such a temper I didn't look where I...was going.'

'Don't panic, Brov! I remember...there're two very tall palm trees...We just go through them... then it's...across a tiny stream...and then it's just a little way to the beach.'

Fergal stumbled and fell.

'Brov!' cried Filly. She knelt beside him. 'Did you hurt yourself?'

'Nope, Sis,' he replied breathlessly. 'It's just that...it's hard to keep up with you ... your legs are longer than mine.'

Suddenly the earth trembled.

The volcano erupted more lava.

Some of it shot so high it seemed to touch the stars.

Burning rocks flew through the air.

'Get on my back, Brov!' yelled Filly.

'But, Sis, I'm too heavy –'

'Don't dilly-zip, Brov!' snapped Filly. 'The whole island is exploding! Chop-zip!'

Fergal climbed on to her back

'Hold tight, Brov!' instructed Filly. And ran. The heat was so intense that Filly could feel her skin tingling.

A rock whizzed past!

It hit a tree!

With a 'woooshing' noise the tree burst into flames!

Filly thought, Where are those two tall palm trees? They were so big...I can't possibly miss them...

'Are we going the right way, Sis?'

'I'm not really sure, Brov...None of these trees looks familiar.'

Wooosh!
Another tree caught fire!
Wooosh! Wooosh!
Two more!
The ground shook again and even more lava gushed from the volcano.
Filly looked behind her.
What she saw nearly made her scream out loud!

The wall of lava was as high as a house. Moving relentlessly forward. Knocking palm trees over as if they were matchsticks. And what's more –

'It's heading straight for us!' gasped Filly, her eyes gleaming with firelight. 'Hold as tight as you can, Brov!'

She ran as fast as she could.

Where are those two tall trees? she thought. Oh, dilly-zip-dally-zip!

There was lava to the left of them now!

They moved to the right.

Wooosh!

A tree caught fire!

Filly looked behind.

The lava was getting closer and closer!

Vrrhhmm! it went.

The air was so thick with heat it was difficult to breathe.

Fergal was coughing.

And then...

Filly saw the two trees!

Both of them were burning...but – yes! – there was just enough space for them to get through.

'Close your eyes, Brov!'

Filly aimed at the gap between the trees, closed her own eyes, and ran –

Flames licked her skin!

Fire roared in her ears!

She tasted smoke on her lips!

But they made it safely through.

'Well done, Sis!'

'Now all we have to do is walk in a straight line, Brov. Not that we have much choice!'

And she was right!

There was still the lava to the left!

And now lava to the right as well!

While behind them, the wall of lava continued to

get closer and closer.

Vrrrhhhmmm!

Filly ran forward. 'Now, there's a tiny stream up here, Brov. We must jump over that and then it's just a little way to the beach.'

Filly stopped running.

She stared ahead.

'Crikey!'

And – for the first time in his life – Fergal uttered 'Crikey!' as well.

For what had been a tiny stream a little while ago was now…a burning river of lava!

And it was no longer tiny!

It was big!

Too big for them to jump over!

'What are we going to do, Sis?'

Filly looked to the left.

Vrrrrhhhhmmmm!

The right!

Vrrrrhhhhmmmm!

Behind!

Vrrrrhhhhmmmm!

And all the lava was getting closer and closer and closer…

We're trapped! thought Filly.

'Now, don't panic, Brov! All we have to do is…'

'Yep, Sis?'

Filly thought for a while, then did the only thing she could think of –

'HELP!' she screamed as loud as she could. 'H-E-L-P!'

'HELP!' screamed Fergal. 'H-E-L-P!'

'I can hear something!' Mrs Thunder exclaimed.

Mr Thunder stopped pushing the timber. He listened for a while.

'Right you are!' he cried. 'It's their voices!'

'But they sound so far away!'

'The wreckage must be muffling everything.' He got his face as close to the cellar door as the timber would allow. 'WE'LL SOON GET YOU OUT! DON'T WORRY, MY KIDDYWINKS!'

And Mrs Thunder called, 'WE'LL SOON BE THERE, MY SWEETHEARTS!'

'FILLY!' called Mrs Love. 'WHERE ARE YOU?'

'FERGAL!' called Mr Love. 'WHERE ARE YOU?'

'WE'RE OVER HERE!' Filly and Fergal yelled.

Then Filly sighed and looked at her brother. 'The volcano is making so much noise, Brov,' she said. 'And with all that lava rumbling and fire crackling...oh, we'll never be heard above it all.'

As if to prove the point, Mr and Mrs Love's voices filtered through to them again.

'WHERE ARE YOU, FILLY?'

'WHERE ARE YOU, FERGAL?'

'WE'RE OVER HERE!'

The lava behind was getting closer and closer. Vrrrrrhhhhhmmmmm!

'Crikey, Brov! Your jumper's smouldering!'

'So is yours, Sis!'

They slapped the smoulding from each other's clothes.

'We're going to be roasted alive, Brov! Oh, where can Mr and Mrs Love be? Don't dilly-chop-zip-dally-zip-chop!'

'Don't panic, Sis!'

'How can I help but panic, Brov! We're surrounded by lava and no one is going to help us and –'

'There!' cried Fergal, pointing. 'There they are!'

Mr and Mrs Love were now on the other side of the lava stream.

'There you are, Filly!' said Mrs Love.

'There you are Fergal!' said Mr Love.

Filly yelled, 'We can't jump over! The stream is too big for us! And...' She looked behind her.

The wall of lava was so close...

'Keep calm!' Mr Love took a few steps back and stared intently at the stream of lava.

'What are you doing?' asked Mrs Love.

'I need a run-up,' replied Mr Love.

'A run-up for what?'

'To leap over the lava.'

'But it's dangerous –'

'It's the only way!' Mr Love looked over at Filly and Fergal. 'Stand back a little,' he called. 'I'll need room to land.'

'Good luck, my love,' said Mrs Love.

And then Mr Love ran!

Ran as fast as he could!

And...jumped!

For one brief moment Filly thought, He's not going to make it! He's going to fall in the lava and –

But he didn't!

Mr Love landed safely beside them.

'That's my muscles on muscles for you! Now, come on, you two! Fergal, you jump on my back. Filly, I'll carry you.'

'Both of us!' exclaimed Filly. 'Are you sure?'

'My muscles can do it!'

'Your eyebrows are singeing, Sis!'

'So are yours, Brov!'

'Quickly, you two!' said Mr Love.

Fergal jumped on his back.

Filly climbed into his arms.

Mr Love went to take a few steps back to get a run-up... but he couldn't!

The heat from the lava was too intense!

'My muscles won't be able to carry you both without a run-up! What shall I do?'

'Take Brov first! I'll wait for you here!'

'Sure, Sis?'

'Positive, Brov!'

'All right, Filly. Get down ... There! I'll be as quick as I can! Hold tight, Fergal!'

Mr Love took a deep breath and jumped

Please make it! thought Filly.

And he did!

He landed on the other side with a solid thump.

Everyone cheered...but only for a second.

'My ankle!' cried Mr Love. 'I've sprained my ankle!' And he lay on the ground, writhing in pain.

'WHAT ABOUT ME?' shouted Filly.

'SIS!'

'BROV!'

Filly's tears turned to steam on her cheeks.

The lava was so close she could spit at it!

Her hair was smoking!

'SIS!'

'BROV!'

And then...

Mrs Love ran at the lava!

'MY LOVE!' cried Mr Love.

Mrs Love jumped...

Please make it! thought Filly.

Mrs Love landed next to Filly and – before anyone had a chance to say anything – she'd picked Filly up and leapt back over again.

'Crikey!' gasped Filly 'That was the most chop-chop leaping I've ever seen!'

The lava was now covering the spot where Filly had just been standing...

Vrrrrrhhhhhmmmmm!

Now it was joining up with the stream of lava!

Vrrrrrrhhhhhhmmmmmm!

'Run!' cried Mrs Love.

'But...my ankle!' whimpered Mr Love. 'I can't walk!'

Mrs Love helped him to his feet. 'Put your arm round my shoulders,' she instructed.

'Ouch!' whined Mr Love as he stepped forward.

The four of them rushed through the jungle.

Still the lava followed them!

'Ouch!'

'Stop complaining, my love!'

'You all right, Sis?'

'Yes, Brov!'

Wooosh! went another tree as it caught fire.

Vrrrrrrrhhhhhhhhmmmmmmmm!

'Ouch!'

Wooosh!

Vrrrrrrrrrhhhhhhhhhmmmmmmmmmmm!

They got to the beach!

'The boat!' cried Mrs Love. 'Quick!'

They ran to the boat!

Mrs Love helped Mr Love inside. 'Now, start rowing!' she said. 'Put those muscles to good use.' Then she reached out to help Filly and Fergal aboard.

'Nope!' said Fergal, stepping back 'We...we can't go with you. Yep, Sis?'

'Right, Brov!'

'But it's not safe here!' Mrs Love told them. 'There won't be any island left in a little while – Look!' She pointed at the birds flying away and the dolphins swimming further out to sea. 'Anything with any sense is leaving!'

The volcano erupted again!

More lava shot into the air!

Vrrrrrrrrrhhhhhhhhhmmmmmmmmmm!

Woooosh!

'We know our own way to get off the island,' insisted Fergal. 'Yep, Sis?'

'Right, Brov!'

'But we'd just *love* you to come with us!' Mrs Love told them. 'Meeting you has made us realize how much...we want a family.'

'I'm glad,' said Fergal. 'But we've got to go...back to where we came from.'

Lava had reached the sand now!

'Start rowing!' cried Filly. 'Quick!'

Mr Love started to row the boat away.

'If you have a boy – ' began Fergal.

'We'll call him Fergal!' Mr and Mrs Love said.

'And a girl?' asked Filly.

'Filly!' came their reply.

The boat was already a long way away.

'Goodbye, Filly and Fergal!'

'Goodbye, Mr and Mrs Love!'

Vrrrrrrrrrrhhhhhhhhhhmmmmmmmmmm!
'Run, Sis!'
They ran across the sand as fast as they could.
Past the heart that Mrs Love had made for Mr Love.
Past the heart that Mr Love had made for Mrs Love.
Past the place where they'd eaten coconuts.
Past the place where they'd first seen dolphins and birds.
'There's the sign!' cried Fergal.
And there it was:

Welcome to Honeymo

The 'ONIA' was already burning!
Filly looked behind.
The lava was flowing over the heart Mrs Love had made for Mr Love.
Vrrrrrrrrrrrhhhhhhhhhhhhmmmmmmmmmmmm!
Over the heart Mr Love had made for Mrs Love.
Vrrrrrrrrrrrhhhhhhhhhhhhmmmmmmmmmmmm!
Over the place where they'd eaten coconuts.
Vrrrrrrrrrrrhhhhhhhhhhhhmmmìmmmmmmmm!
Over the place where they'd first seen dolphins and birds.
Vrrrrrrrrrrrhhhhhhhhhhhhmmmmmmmmmmmm!
Lava had reached the sea now!
Hisssss! went the water as the red-hot lava turned it to steam.
And that's when they saw the entrance to the tunnel!
'Quick, Brov!'
Vrrrrrrrrrhhhhhhhhhhmmmmmmmmmm!
Wooooossshhh!
Hisssssssss!

Filly and Fergal ran into the tunnel!
And the wooshing got fainter.
And the hissing got fainter.
But not the vrrrhhhmmming!
In fact…it got louder!
Filly looked behind.
The lava had followed them into the tunnel!
And it was moving faster than ever!

VRRRRRRRHHHHHHHHHHMMMMMMMM!

'HELP!' screamed Filly.
'HELP!' screamed Fergal.

'Hear that?' gasped Mrs Thunder. 'Their voices are much louder now!'

Mr Thunder nodded. 'I heard.'

Both of them were dripping with sweat and caked with dirt now.

'They're calling for help!' said Mrs Thunder. Then she called, 'DON'T WORRY, SWEETHEARTS!'

'One...two...three...Push!' urged Mr Thunder. Then called, 'DON'T WORRY, KIDDYWINKS!'

Together they pushed the timber.

With creaking sounds, it continued to move.

'WE'RE GETTING THERE, SWEETHEARTS!'

'WE'RE GETTING THERE, KIDDYWINKS!'

'That's Mum!' declared Filly.

'And Dad!' declared Fergal.

They had just reached the cellar.

Behind them, the lava was making its way down the tunnel.

'Crikey!'

Filly rushed up the stairs and tried to open the cellar door.

'It still won't budge, Brov!'

'Look, Sis!'

VRRRRRRRHHHHHHHHHMMMMMMMM!

'Crikey! It's going to come in here after us...MUM! DAD! GET THE DOOR OPEN, QUICK!...They'll do it, Brov! Get up here with me! You want to be as far from the hole as possible, Brov!'

Fergal rushed up the steps and clutched Filly.

The lava was almost in the cellar now!

VRRRRRRRHHHHHHHHHMMMMMMMM!

The cellar was getting hotter and hotter!

And redder and redder!

'We're going to be cooked, Sis!'

'Fried, Brov!'

'Roasted, Sis!'

'Grilled, Brov!'

Hotter and hotter!

Redder and redder!

Sweat trickled down Filly's face.

Sweat tricked down Fergal's face.

VRRRRRRRHHHHHHHHHMMMMMMMM!

'MUM!' screamed Filly. 'SAVE US!'

'DAD!' screamed Fergal. 'SAVE US!'

'Of course we'll save you, sweethearts!'

'Of course we'll save you, kiddywinks!'

And, with one almighty heave, they pushed the timber out of the way.

It crashed to the ground!

Dust billowed everywhere!

Mr Thunder grabbed the cellar door!

Mrs Thunder grabbed the cellar door!

And, together, they...

'The door's opening!' cried Filly.

'And the lava's here!' cried Fergal.

VRRRRRRRRHHHHHHHHHHHMMMMMMMMM!

This is it! thought Filly. The bubbling lava is going to fill up the cellar! Then go up the stairs! And then it's going to start spreading all over The Surface of the Moon!

VRRRRR –

But that's not what happened!

The lava didn't flow into the cellar at all!

It stopped at the entrance and...filled the hole up!

Filly thought, It's as if there's a sheet of glass in front of the hole. The lava's just piling up behind it!

Everything went very quiet

So quiet, in fact, that the only sound to be heard for a while was the 'thump-thump' of Filly and Fergal's hearts.

Then there were other sounds...

'There you are, my kiddiwinks!'

'There you are, my sweethearts!'

Mr and Mrs Thunder had opened the cellar door!
'Mum and Dad!'

Filly and Fergal rushed out of the cellar into the arms of their parents.

There was a lot of hugging and kissing. And, although it might not have been the most hugging and kissing in The Whole History of Hugging and Kissing, it was certainly the most hugging and kissing to have ever been seen in the Thunder house.

Except, of course, it wasn't a house any more. It was just a pile of –

'Rubble!' gasped Filly, looking round her. 'Wh…what happened!'

The sun was rising now and Filly and Fergal could see the remains of the house.

'It fell down, sweetheart,' explained Mrs Thunder.

'But how?' Filly wanted to know.

'Your mum and I slammed the front door too

hard,' replied Mr Thunder, 'and...well...'

'All the cracks joined up, didn't they, Dad?'

Mr Thunder nodded.

'I had a feeling they'd do that one day,' sighed Filly.

There was a slight pause.

'We found...*The Book of Arguments*, sweetheart,' said Mrs Thunder softly.

'Crikey! You weren't supposed to see that!'

'I'm glad we did, my kiddywink,' said Mr Thunder. 'Because your mum and I have got something to tell you –'

'I'VE GOT SOMETHING TO TELL YOU FIRST!' interrupted Fergal, loudly and firmly. 'YOU TWO ARE NOT GOING TO ARGUE ANY MORE! ME AND SIS ARE FED UP WITH IT ALL! WE'RE FED UP WITH LISTENING TO ALL THE INSULTS AND THINGS BREAKING! WE'RE FED UP WITH HAVING TO GLUE THINGS BACK TOGETHER! WE'RE FED UP WITH MUM CALLING DAD "NINCOMPOOP" AND DAD CALLING MUM "NUMBSKULL"! WE'RE FED UP WITH YOU TWO SAYING YOU WANT A DIVORCE ALL THE TIME! AND WE'RE FED UP WITH TRYING TO MAKE OUT YOUR ARGUING WAS OUR HOBBY! BECAUSE HOBBIES ARE SUPPOSED TO BE FUN, AND LISTENING TO YOU TWO SHOUT AT EACH OTHER ALL DAY LONG IS NOT FUN AT ALL! WELL, IT'S GOING TO STOP! BECAUSE, IF IT DOESN'T ... *WE'LL DIVORCE YOU!*'

Mr and Mrs Thunder were flabbergasted!

They'd only ever heard Fergal say two words at a time before. And never to them anyway. And now...now this! They stared at him with their mouths open.

Gradually Mrs Thunder got over her shock.

'But...but, my sweetheart,' she began, 'that's just

what we were about to tell you. Your dad and I...well, we're so sorry for all the arguments. We've been silly and selfish. It won't happen again. We promise you. Your dad and I love each other very much. And we both love you very much. From now on...we'll be a happy family!'

'Wonderful!' declared Fergal. 'Perhaps that means we can get something to eat at last. Steak and chips would go down nicely. Yep, Sis?'

'Right, Brov!'

'Anything you want, my sweethearts!'

'Anything at all, my kiddywinks!'

And they all started hugging and kissing again.

Yes, thought Filly. Things are really going to be different from now on. I can feel it. After all, I am an expert on arguing parents, so I should recognize unarguing ones when I see them.

Then a new sound filled the air...

Whistling!

It was the postman.

He was strolling towards them, looking all round.

'Do you know where the Thunder family live?' he asked.

'We're the Thunder family,' Mr Thunder told him.'And we live here. Or, rather, we did. Our house fell down last night.'

'Must have been in the stars,' the postman said. 'Anyway, I've got a letter for you lot.'

The postman handed the letter over, then strolled away, still whistling.

They opened the letter and read:

Dear Mr and Mrs Thunder

We're so sorry it's taken us such a long time to build your new house. It must have been terrible for you living amongst all that rubble, with no neighbours to talk to and no friends for your two lovely children to play with.

But now we're glad to tell you – the waiting is over!

Your new house is built and we want you to come and live in it as soon as possible. It's a very beautiful house and it has a garden and a road outside where you can park your car.

Now, I know what you're thinking – We can't afford a car! But don't worry! You soon will! There're lots of jobs here, you see, so you'll soon be able to own a set of wheels. And lots of other things besides.

Your new neighbours can't wait to meet you. And all the children are looking forward to making friends with Filly and Fergal.

Once again, we're sorry for the long delay...but these things just happen!

Best wishes,

The Powers that Be

'A new house!' cried Mrs Thunder.

'And a new job!' cried Mr Thunder.

'And friends!' cried Filly and Fergal.

And – you've guessed it! – they started hugging and kissing each other all over again.

'We need a new lamp,' said Mrs Thunder.

'And a new washing-machine,' said Mr Thunder.

'And a new telephone.'

'And a new spin-drier.'

'And a new television.'

And Mr and Mrs Thunder talked on and on about all the things they were going to get and do. And, now and again, they called each other 'my love' and kissed. But not too much. Just enough to show they truly meant it.

Filly and Fergal sat next to each other.

'Honeymoonia will be our secret, Sis,' said Fergal.

'Right, Brov.'

'No one will ever believe us anyway, Sis.'

'Right, Brov.'

'And as for the meteorite spoo – The spoon!'

Fergal jumped up and rushed down to the cellar. A moment later he returned, holding the spoon.

'I don't think we need that any more, Brov,' Filly told him. 'Look at Mum and Dad. The arguments are over.'

'I know that, Sis. But I want to take the spoon with us to our new house.'

'Why, Brov?' asked Filly.

'Because we might meet another child like we were. Someone whose parents argue all the time. There must be hundreds of children like that out there, Sis.'

'Thousands, Brov.'

'Millions, Sis.'

'Billions, Brov.'

'Trillions, Sis.'

'Zillions, Brov.'

'Squillions, Sis. And when I do meet one of the squillions of children, I'm going to give him or her the meteorite spoon. And you know what I'll say, Sis?'

'What, Brov?'

'I'll say, "Be brave, my chickling, be brave!"'